SUE BARTON – STAFF NURSE

Dr Warren unfolded his long length from the chair, found his head on a level with Nancy's, clasped her melodramatically in his arms and kissed her – warmly.

Nancy emerged slightly rumpled from his embrace, said demurely, 'Thank you kindly, sir,', picked up the stool, replaced it in the linen closet, and went on her way, laughing.

Sue was the only one who had seen Margot Harrison come down the corridor just as Frank had kissed Nancy the second time. She had halted, frozen, until Nancy stooped to retrieve the stool.

Then she fled.

Sue Barton – Staff Nurse

Helen Dore Boylston

KNIGHT BOOKS
Hodder and Stoughton

First published in England by The Bodley Head Ltd 1953

This edition first published by Knight Books 1970

Fifth impression 1979

Printed and bound in Great Britain for
Hodder and Stoughton Paperbacks, a
division of Hodder and Stoughton Ltd.,
Mill Road, Dunton Green, Sevenoaks,
Kent (Editorial Office: 47 Bedford
Square, London, WC1 3DP) by
Hunt Barnard Printing Ltd.,
Aylesbury, Bucks.

ISBN 0 340 04010 6

Contents

1	No shadow	*page*	7
2	Sunday night		15
3	Nothing serious?		23
4	Practical and definite		28
5	Denham Two		35
6	'A nice boy and a good doctor, but—'		53
7	Day off		70
8	When a good nurse makes a mistake		76
9	Nurses		91
10	The remainder		100
11	Everybody's troubles		108
12	Young lady with lamp		117
13	Mistletoe		126
14	New Year's Eve		134
15	Miss Van Dyke's position		143
16	St Valentine's Day		149

I

No shadow

THAT Friday seemed like every other July day and not at all like an end to anything. Great puffs of white cloud drifted innocently across the hazy summit of Mt Washington, the afternoon was drowsy with the songs of insects and the smell of pines. A breeze, fresh and clean from the wooded slopes of New Hampshire's Presidential Range, brought a pleasant touch of coolness. It was a day to enjoy and there was no hint of trouble in it.

Sue paused halfway up the back-porch steps and turned, a slender figure in white slacks and green blouse. Her copper-red hair was brushed softly back from a vivid face which refused to tan regardless of sun and wind, and her brown eyes were quiet with contentment. She smiled, half in tenderness, half in amusement, as she looked back.

Her five-year-old twins, Johnny and Jerry, with Maxl the dachshund, were entangled in a wriggling heap on the lawn. Her daughter Tabitha, aged seven, was swinging under the big maple, dark pigtails flying as she swooped. From the tool shed came a bass rumble slightly off key – the voice of Sue's husband, Dr William Barry, humming Old Man River while he collected his fishing kit. Indoors and somewhat muffled by distance Sue heard a gurgle followed by a prolonged squeak and she laughed. The baby was awake.

The late afternoon sunlight spilled down through the

maples, touching into brilliance the red heads of the tumbling little boys, and dappling Tabitha's happy face.

Last July, Sue remembered – transporting herself back a year in order to enjoy the feeling of having a second sight – last July at this time Tabitha had been going through a hurt-feeling phase. Jerry had been behaving like a problem child for the very good reason that he had exceptional musical talent which nobody suspected. Johnny, the practical, had fallen violently in love. Caroline Stuart, a teen-age neighbour, was having serious trouble at home, and both she and her mother were appealing to Sue for help.

It was like trying to walk five tightropes at once, Sue thought, especially with my own state of mind making everything more difficult.

Her state of mind, that summer, had been induced by a growing sense of guilt because her training as a nurse and her experience in hospital and public health work were growing rusty with disuse – were, Sue felt, being wasted. When the children were babies it had been all right, but now that they were school age she could, and *should* be working – or so she thought. The matter had troubled her for months, until she finally told Bill about it. What he said had helped a lot, but the coming of Baby Sue had helped most of all.

If she still had an occasional fit of restlessness, she no longer felt guilty. She was doing the most important job there was, right here; Bill had convinced her of that, and Baby Sue made short work of the restless moments. There ought, always, to be a baby in the house, Sue thought – and went indoors, to find her youngest cradled in the arms of a stout, white-haired woman with serene eyes – Veazie Ann Cooney, an old friend and now Sue's housekeeper.

Veazie Ann was sitting comfortably in the kitchen rocker, the remains of the baby's supper on a small table beside her. The baby was more than comfortable, she was ecstatic, though her mouth and chin had disappeared behind clots and smears of crimson. Both cheeks were mottled with a repellent brown substance of the consistency of mud, and one eyebrow dripped red.

'Good heavens!' said her mother. 'She looks like a traffic accident. Did *any* of the liver or tomato go *into* her mouth?'

'Sartin. Most of 'em. But she ain't real restrained about her meals. Kind of goes to meet 'em.'

'You call that a meeting? I'd call it a head-on collision. You needn't have fed her, Veazie Ann. I was coming right in.'

'I enjoy feeding her.' Veazie Ann wiped a splotch of tomato out of the baby's hair. 'Land, Sue, she's the image of ye. She's a-going to be like ye, too. Seems as though this one's more yourn than any of the others.'

Sue smiled down at the red-gold fuzz on her daughter's head. 'Could be,' she admitted, 'but it's a little hard to say at four months.' She turned at the sound of Bill's step. 'Hello! All ready to go?'

'Sure.'

He came to grin at the baby, his tall figure and broad shoulders enormous beside her small pinkness.

'Hi, Shrimp,' he said.

The baby gurgled and held out her arms, her tiny starfish hands as daubed with liver and tomato as her face.

Bill backed away. 'Oh, no!' he said. 'I've got a moustache already – and it doesn't need decorating.' He tickled her gently in the stomach and she squeaked with pleasure. Then her eyes closed and she slept, instantly, replete with food, warmth and contentment – the sudden sleep of the very young.

'Wow!' said her father, admiringly. 'That's a talent I wish I had. I could do with it.'

Sue glanced at him quickly. 'Why?' she asked. 'Aren't you sleeping?'

'Oh, sure – but I still seem to be all in, most of the time.'

'I thought you said things had been rather easy at the hospital this last month.'

'They have – but I've got a practice, too, you know.' He went to the sink, turned on the tap, picked up a bar of laundry soap, and began to lather his hands and arms, his movements so automatically those of a surgeon scrubbing for an operation that Sue grinned.

Veazie Ann rose with the sleeping baby. 'I'll fix her, Sue,' she said. 'Don't you bother. You get Bill off to a good start.' She went away, moving softly.

Sue leaned against the sink, looking at Bill with sharply professional eyes. He did look tired, but she had never known a doctor who didn't.

'Can't you take more than two days off?' she asked suddenly.

'Nope. Got an operation scheduled for eight a.m. Monday.' He rinsed off the soap and looked around expectantly.

'You're home, now, darling. Remember?' said Sue, handing him a towel.

Bill's deep-set blue eyes laughed into hers as he dried his hands. 'So I am! And the lack of respect I get around here is –'

'Does you good! Doctors are spoiled to death in a hospital. "Yes, sir." "No, sir." "Oh, yes, certainly, Doctor." '

'Go on! It's, "Oh, please, Doctor – couldn't that dressing

wait — we're just getting out the supper trays." "But Doctor, the lumbar puncture set hasn't come back from the sterilizing room." "Oh, Doctor — but I've only got *two* nurses on the floor, and we're rushed to death — I don't see how —" '

'All right, you win,' said Sue, laughing. She hung the damp towel on the rack. 'Will you be home in time for supper, Sunday night?'

Bill considered. 'I don't know,' he said at last. 'If they're biting we won't. If they aren't we will — unless Ira has some other plan. Anyhow, we *will* be back by dark, that's sure. What are you going to do?'

'Oh, nothing in particular. Kit's coming over. She's got the week-end off. What time is Ira coming for you?'

'Now,' said Bill, looking through the side kitchen window.

'Mercy! Have you got everything? Enough food? Toothbrush? Change of clothes in case you get wet? Bread? Flour —'

'Linen? Silver? My dinner jacket?' He flung an arm around Sue, kissed her heartily, said, ' 'Bye, Sweetheart,' and was gone before she could reply.

She went out on the porch, but he was already across the lawn with the children trailing behind, and she halted. 'Do be careful!' she shouted, and waved at Ira Prouty, who was loading the car, called to the children — who didn't hear her — and waved again when the car drove away.

As the sound of the engine died in the distance, her attention was caught by a low rumble and she turned, following the sound, which came from the west. A great silver-headed, anvil-shaped cloud was swelling above the horizon, a streamer of white fanning out from it.

Golly! Sue thought, turning back into the house.

It's going to be a bad storm. I hope Bill reaches camp first.

It *was* a bad one, when it finally struck some time later. Wind raged and blue-black clouds boiled overhead, split again and again by forked lightning. The house was drowned with rain and rocked with thunder, and Sue hoped again that Bill and Ira were safe in their dry warm little cabin; it was comfortably furnished, well stocked with canned goods, and had an excellent stove. If they were wet when they reached it they would soon dry out. But they should have reached it – or almost. It wasn't too far away as the crow flew – ten miles by road. But there would be five miles to go on foot, over a faint trail through the woods to a roaring stream on whose banks they had built the cabin.

Sue had been there only once, but once was enough, and as she turned her attention to preparations for the children's baths she tried not to think of Bill's favourite fishing spot, a deep icy whirlpool with wicked-looking rocks jutting out of the white water.

'Honestly,' she said to Kit the next day, 'the things men go through to capture a few frantically reluctant fish! Crashing through five miles of briars with packs on their backs – the men, I mean, not the briars – and then, after they've thrashed and struggled up and down all day in that terrifying stream, and have been eaten to the marrow by bugs, they have to come back to that cabin and *cook dinner!*'

'It's fun,' said Kit lazily. 'It's perfectly gorgeous there, and besides, they *like* fishing, which makes all the difference. I like it, myself.'

'I know you do. You and Bill are both wacky.'

The conversation lapsed into the pleasant silence of a very old companionship, as indeed it was, for Sue and Katherine Van Dyke had been in the same class in their nursing school and had worked together at the Henry Street Visiting Nurse Service in New York. Later, when Sue, then engaged to Bill, had come to the little village of Springdale in the White Mountains to work as Public Health Nurse while Bill started his practice, Kit had joined her. Then, when Sue and Bill were married and had achieved their dream of having a hospital in Springdale, Sue had resigned after three years as Director of Nurses, and Kit had taken her place.

It all seemed like a minute, Sue mused, the way the years telescoped together as one grew older, and the funny part of it was, you didn't feel older.

She glanced at Kit, stretched out in a lawn chair in the shade of a giant elm behind the house. Kit didn't seem any older, and how she managed to look smart in an old faded cotton dress, Sue didn't know, except that Kit wore any clothes well, and despite the fact that the children had been climbing all over her, she was still trim and un-rumpled. Her brown hair was smooth, her slightly uptilted nose was cheerful, her brown eyes regarded the world impudently from beneath high-arched brows. She was fun to have around.

Sue leaned back and looked up at the clear, rain-washed sky.

'I do hope,' she said suddenly, and for the tenth time, 'that Bill and Ira got to the cabin before that storm hit yesterday.'

'For heaven's sake, what's the matter with you, Sue? You never used to go into these worrying fits. A little rain-water isn't going to melt Bill.'

'I know,' Sue agreed. 'I don't know why I'm worrying. Is that the baby yelling?'

Kit grinned. 'You're darned right, it is. Shall I go and get her?'

'The pleasure is all yours.' Then, as Kit rose, Sue added, 'Nappies included.'

'You wouldn't be hinting, would you?'

'Certainly.' Sue closed her eyes in comfortable relaxation while she considered various agreeable small plans. The children would love a picnic lunch on the lawn, and later this afternoon they could all go berrying. Everybody would enjoy that: the children because it was an adventure, Kit because she'd like being out of doors and doing something, and Sue because she loved the plunk of berries dropping into a pail, and the smell of sweetfern and warm underbrush. Besides, it was oddly satisfying to provide out of the lavishness of fields and woods – good food to be had for the taking. Sue's mouth watered, thinking of blueberry muffins and raspberry pie. As for tomorrow – well, tomorrow could take care of itself.

She smiled, listening to Kit's voice talking nonsense to the baby. It was going to be a nice week-end in spite of Bill's absence, which seemed to leave gaps in all kinds of unexpected ways.

It *was* a nice week-end; so nice, in fact, that Sue always remembered it, not because anything in particular happened, but because that Saturday, and Sunday until late evening, in their blend of busyness, tranquillity, and laughter, were so typical of everything that was best in a very happy phase of her life.

2

Sunday night

THE telephone continued to ring, with the dogged persistence customary in rural communities where people must run down from the attic, up from the cellar, or in from the garden.

Sue, in this instance, was involved with a plate of cold roast beef which refused to go all the way into the refrigerator, and remained obstinately half in and half out. Kit was upstairs reading to the children before they went to sleep, and Veazie Ann had gone to a neighbour's for the evening. Sue finally yanked the plate out, all but hurled it on to the kitchen table, and dashed into the hall – feeling, unreasonably, that people ought to find out what she was doing before they telephoned her.

She snatched up the receiver and said 'Hello' with a detached courtesy which, in her own ears, sounded revoltingly hypocritical.

'That you, Sue?' a voice demanded. It was Marianna Prouty, Ira's wife.

Marianna was not a native of Springdale, having been born almost literally in the gutters of New York, and her speech, once pure Lower East Side, had, since her marriage to Ira, become a curious mixture of New Yorkese and rural New Hampshire.

'Ira there?' she went on.

'Why, no,' said Sue, surprised. 'Bill didn't really expect to get home before dark.'

'Well, *Ira* did. Geeze, Sue, he's gotta! We got fifteen cows to milk. The Wilkins boy come over and done it Friday and Saturday, but he *told* Ira he couldn't come tonight – and there ain't anybody else. Ira said he'd be home sure by milking time.' She added with the gruffness which, in Marianna, stood for apology, 'I can't milk. Gotta bad hand. The baby slammed the icebox door on it.'

'Oh, no! I'm so sorry. Is it bad?'

'Ayuh,' Marianna said briefly, 'Mashed a couple fingers. But Sue, when Ira says he's gonna do something – he does it. And he ain't – so I know something's happened. What ya think we better do?'

Sue had always been uneasy when Bill was away on one of his fishing trips, and now, for the space of a breath, she was frightened. Then common sense came to her rescue.

'Don't worry, Marianna. They're all right. Very likely they've had a flat tyre – or maybe they were late starting back.'

' 'Twouldn't take till now to fix a flat, an' Ira wouldn't be late starting – not with fifteen cows a-waitin' for him and bawling the place down.'

'Well, maybe the car wouldn't start,' said Sue patiently, for the men had gone in Ira's ancient farm truck which was known to have its little ways, all of them perverse.

Marianna, however, was not convinced. 'No,' she insisted. 'If it was that old goat of a truck Ira woulda called me. After all, they leave it, right there at Cass's Corners. I'm tellin' you they're still back *in* there.'

The ominous quality of this last remark had its effect on Sue in spite of herself, and her reply was more irritable than she intended.

'For heaven's sake, Marianna! There are dozens of things that could have delayed them, no matter how much Ira wanted to get back.'

'Well – what?'

'Goodness! How should I know? They might have gone farther from camp than they intended – Bill especially – and they don't usually stay together. Ira would have to wait for Bill. Or maybe the car broke down along that stretch coming home where there aren't any houses. After all, cars love to do things like that. There are lots of –'

'Yeah; there sure are! Maybe somebody's got a busted leg – or – fell in that pool –'

'Nonsense!' said Sue sharply. 'If one of them got hurt the other would come out to the Corners and telephone. Stop worrying.'

'Oh, sure. Easy as pie. So what do I do with these dratted cows? You want me to get one in so you can talk to it on the phone an' explain why it ain't gonna be milked?'

Sue grinned. 'No cow has ever believed a word I've said, about anything. They're allergic to me. But I'll tell you what, I'll call up around here and send somebody over to milk for you. Then, if Bill and Ira aren't here by dark we can decide what to do. All right?'

'I – I guesso. Well, so long – and thanks.'

Sue remained at the telephone until she had located two neighbouring farmers' sons who could be spared to milk Ira's cows, and who had a car to take them to the lonely hillside farm. Then she went into the living room and sat down in the big armchair by the window, stretching herself out at full length. But the mood of warm contentment, which had made the week-end so happy, was gone.

She stared out at the bright sky, trying to recapture that sense of well-being, and found only a growing uncertainty.

The open lawn around the house still seemed in full daylight, but trees and shrubbery were already dim and unreal, and their shadowiness was reflected in Sue's eyes. What could have happened? Something *must* have, or Ira would be at home by this time. Sue hoped it was the truck, but as she watched the gathering darkness the accumulated anxiety of years gathered with it and fell upon her, and by the time Kit came downstairs Sue had progressed beyond any uncertainty.

'Everybody's settled,' Kit said cheerfully. 'Hey! What's the matter with you? You look like a city dump in the rain.'

Sue explained.

'Oh, don't be an idiot,' Kit said. 'Of course, they're all right. You've just been listening to Marianna and her cows.'

'Maybe. But all the same, I never did like these expeditions. What *is* it about men that makes them dote on violent effort and hair-breadth escapes?'

'Rapid metabolism,' said Kit comfortably. 'And a good thing too. We'd be in a fine mess if they didn't have it.'

'I don't care. I don't like this.'

'Oh, go on! I'll bet you anything Bill and Ira will turn up here safe and sound within the next ten minutes.'

The minutes, however, crawled past: ten – fifteen – half an hour – and there was still no sign of the truck. Sue had tried to relax, but by quarter to nine, she stopped pretending. The only light outside, now, was in the faintly luminous sky. Sue dropped the book she was not reading and stood up.

'I'm going to call Lot Phinney,' she said abruptly, and this time Kit only nodded.

Lot Phinney had been the town's First Selectman for many years – a wise, kindly, blunt old man who had been

Sue's friend from the day she arrived in Springdale. She turned to him now, instinctively, thankful for the sound of his irritable voice saying, 'Who is it an' what ye want?'

'It's Sue, Lot. I – I'm a little worried, and I thought you'd know what would be the best thing to do.' She told him what had happened, and when she had finished there was a brief silence at the end of the wire.

'Hm,' Lot said at last. ' 'Tain't like Ira, an' that's a fact. Tell ye what – s'pos'n I call up Bige Cass. He can find out if the truck's still there. If 'tain't – well an' good. If 'tis, then Bige or his oldest boy can go in to the cabin a-horse-back an' see what's a-goin' on. I'll let ye know the minute I hear. Jest don't git all het up, Sue. No use a-borrowin' trouble.'

Sue reflected ungratefully that there was nothing like a good old saying for *not* cheering you up, but she thanked Lot and settled herself to wait for his return call. After an interminable fifteen minutes he confirmed her suspicion that trouble had definitely not been borrowed.

'The truck's still there, Sue,' he said. 'Bige is a-goin' in himself. 'Twun't take too long on that colt of his'n. An' you better leave me tell Marianna. If she's got the high-strikes it'll be kinder hard on you.'

Sue was surprised at the steadiness of her own voice. 'How long do you think it will be, before we'll hear?'

'Dunno, exactly – 'bout an hour – maybe less.'

Sue thanked him and went back to the living room. She was not conscious of the coldness of her hands or the dryness of her mouth; she merely wondered why she didn't seem to feel anything, and could tell Kit in a calm, every-day voice what Lot had said.

Kit, after one look at Sue's colourless face, decided to refrain from comment, discussion, or speculation; and so, in a wordless understanding, they did the dishes. They changed the baby, taking comfort from her fat legs and sleepy murmurs. Kit called the Prouty farm, offering to drive over for Marianna and the baby if Marianna wanted to wait at Sue's. Marianna replied gloomily that she didn't.

Veazie Ann came home and Kit explained to her, but for once Veazie Ann had little to offer in the way of reassurance – beyond saying, 'The worse ye expect things to be, the more likely 'tis they'll turn out all right. Where's Sue?'

'Out on the porch.'

They found her pacing up and down. 'I'm sorry to be so fidgety,' she said to Kit. 'It must be like spending the week-end with a caged leopard.'

They were grinning at each other wanly when the telephone rang with what seemed to everybody a peculiar urgency. Sue fled to answer it, leaving Kit and Veazie Ann staring at one another in silent apprehension.

It was Lot, and he answered Sue's breathless 'Hello' with a simple statement of facts.

'Bige is back, Sue. They're in there, all right, but there warn't any accident. Bill's sick.'

'Sick! *What is it?*'

'Pneumony. Leastways, that's what Bill told Ira.'

'Pneumonia!' Sue repeated. She sat down abruptly in the chair by the telephone table. 'Oh!' she said, but there was relief in her voice, as well as distress. 'Why didn't Ira let us know? How long has he been sick?'

'Sence yesterday afternoon. But seems – now don't git scared, Sue – seems the Doc's kind of out of his head. Keeps a'seein' the darnedest things, an' wun't stay quiet. Ira was scairt to leave him.'

'I see,' quietly. 'Well, we've got to get him out of there as quickly as possible. Pneumonia is easy to handle if it doesn't go too long. Is he having any pain?'

'Considerable, I should judge. Ira told Bige the Doc was up and down and a-tossin' all the time. Can't seem to sleep or git fixed so he can breathe easy.'

'Lobar,' said Sue automatically. 'I'll call the hospital right away.'

'Hold on, now, Sue. Best git the State Police ambulance. Bill's a big man and them State Troopers is a husky lot. Anyway, they'll need four to lug him out. You want I should call 'em?'

'Please. And will you tell them to take oxygen, just in case – and to stop at the hospital for Dr Mason. Then I'd like to have them pick me up, here.'

'You ain't a-goin' way in there, Sue? They's no need. They'll git him out all right.'

'I know they will, but I'm going, all the same.' She added under her breath, 'Try and stop me.'

Lot, however, didn't try. He had known Sue for a long time. 'Well,' he said, 'have it your own way – ye will, anyhow. I'll call the State barracks. G'bye.' He hung up before Sue could thank him.

She turned, to find Kit and Veazie Ann in the hall doorway.

'I heard,' Kit said. 'Lucky it's no worse.'

Sue nodded, her professional mind in full charge of her emotions, and busy with details as she called the hospital and asked for Dr Mason, the medical resident.

He listened without comment to Sue's story. Then he said, 'Right, I'll be ready. He's going to need a couple of shots before he starts out. And I'll tell the Front Office to have a room ready.'

Sue hesitated. 'But – I thought – why couldn't he be sick at home?'

'Better not, Mrs Barry. He must be pretty dehydrated by this time. He'll have to have infusions – and he may need oxygen. Besides, this is his hospital and – er – it would look sort of funny if he didn't – I mean –'

'Of course,' Sue agreed. 'I'm sorry. I'm afraid I was only thinking about him as my husband. But I'll be specialing him tonight in any case, so if you'll tell the night supervisor –'

'Sure. Okay. Be seeing you.'

Sue rose, just as Kit came down the front stairs with Sue's blue Visiting Nurse's uniform over one arm.

'I'll take this along for you,' Kit said. 'I'll grant you it's not orthodox, but you simply can't special Bill in slacks.'

'Sue,' said Veazie Ann, 'there's hot coffee ready.'

Sue gulped the coffee, snatched a coat, and was out in the driveway, calling back over her shoulder, 'Let Marianna know, will you, please?' when the blinking red lights of the police ambulance came up the hill and turned in at the lane.

3

Nothing serious?

IRA gave Sue the essentials of what had happened while they were tramping through the darkness behind the slow stretcher. The details he filled in two days later in the sun porch outside Bill's hospital room.

The whole thing, Ira thought, had started with the thunderstorm on Friday. 'She bust loose on us, a-rainin' pitchforks, when we was about half a mile in. Like to of drowned us both. We was soaked and Bill seemed awful tired, right from the beginnin'. Gen'rally he rips along that trail like all git-out, but this time he took it slow, rain or no rain. 'Twarn't like him. You figger he was sick a'ready?'

'I don't know,' said Sue slowly. 'I don't think so. He's been tired like that for months.'

'Well, howsumever, his teeth was a-chatterin' long afore we reached the cabin, an' when we did 'twas damper'n a toad's stommick in there. I fixed a fire in the stove and give him some hot coffee, an' after that he seemed all right.'

Bill had been all right the next day, too. In fact, he had seemed in unusually good spirits. They had made some sandwiches for lunch, and had gone their separate ways, not meeting until supper-time, at the cabin, both with good catches of trout.

'He was fine, then,' Ira said, 'for all he was soakin' wet agin – said he slipped on a rock, mid-stream, 'round noon-time. He was hoppin' mad because it spiled his sand-wiches He et a big dinner.'

'In *wet clothes*?'

'Lordy, no! He put on a pair of overhalls an' a sweater I'd left there from last time. They was kinder spidery an' too small, and he looked like Willie off the yacht in 'em – but they was dry.'

After supper, however, Bill had spoken again of being tired and both men had gone to bed early. Bill had fallen asleep at once.

It was at some time after midnight that Ira had been awakened by the sound of Bill's voice. *He was talking to himself*. Ira had put on his flashlight, and had found Bill huddled under the blankets shaking with a violent chill. It had lasted a long time despite the fact that Ira had piled his own blankets on Bill and had tucked a cider jug filled with boiling water into the bed.

'Soon's I lit the lamp an' commenced hustlin' around he knew where he was, an' he made sense, a-talkin' to me. But he was havin' a time a-breathin', an' when the chill finally quit he was a-burnin' up. He knew right off 'twas the pneumony. I hope I done the right things, Sue.'

'Nobody could have done better,' Sue assured him truthfully.

Bill had told Ira to go out to Cass's Corners and tele-phone Sue, but this had proved impossible.

'I hadn't no more'n lit the lantern an' pulled on a sweater than he was outer bed an' a-stalkin' somethin' over in a corner acrost the cabin. Said 'twas a thing in a long cloak with a hood an' he didn't like the way it kep a' looking at him without no face.'

Sue gave a faint moan in spite of herself and Ira glanced at her quickly. 'You sure you want I should tell you all this, Sue? After all, it's over now, an' he's gettin' on fine. They's no need to –'

'Yes there *is*,' said Sue firmly. 'I want to *know*.'

So Ira went on with his story. He had put the lighted lantern where it illuminated the suspicious corner, and Bill returned docilely to his bunk.

'But in about five minutes he got the notion either the cabin or the woods was afire. Claimed the room was full of smoke, though 'twarn't – an 'he was all for gittin' outer there straight off. So you see I couldn't leave him.'

'No, you certainly couldn't. Oh, dear, if I'd *only* known! I suppose there wasn't even an aspirin tablet in the place.'

'Well, there was – in the First Aid kit – an' I kep a-givin' 'em to him, but I might's well of give him spruce gum for all the good they did.'

'They may have kept his temperature from going any higher. And I'm sure they helped the pain.'

'Think so? Gosh, I hope they done somethin' for him – poor cuss. But 'twas funny, Sue – for all he was crazy as a coot half the time, t'other half he was real sensible. He see, himself, I couldn't leave him, but he said no matter, because when we didn't show up, Sunday night, you'd start a-makin' the fur fly. Said you had the best judgment of any woman he ever knew in his life.'

'He said that?' Sue blinked back sudden tears. 'But – anybody would have done exactly the same thing that I did, in this case.'

'I dunno's they would, Sue. 'Twas good judgment callin' Lot Phinney. There's plenty would of been just rarin' round screechin' ... Anyhow, he wanted I should keep a-pourin' water into him – whether he wanted it or no. So I done it all Sunday, till 'twas a wonder he didn't float off the bunk.'

'That did him more good than anything, Ira. I can't tell you how grateful I am – for everything.'

'Shucks,' said Ira, his lean face suddenly crimson. 'You figger he's all right now, Sue? He don't seem very comfortable. What makes him spit that bloody-looking stuff?'

'That's typical of lobar pneumonia. But he's all right. He doesn't need a special, even. This is my last day. Of course, his temperature still goes up in the late afternoon, but it's not important and it won't do that much longer.'

Ira accepted this statement with complete faith in Sue's knowledge of illness, and left the hospital much relieved.

Bill's temperature, however, continued to rise in the afternoons and, long after he should have been well enough to finish his convalescence at home, he was kept on at the hospital – until one day, when Sue came over for her afternoon visit, she was startled to see a nurse's isolation gown and mask hanging just inside the door.

She stared. '*What* –' she began indignantly.

'Sit down, darling,' Bill said gently. 'No, over there – and don't kiss me.'

He told her why, trying not to see the sudden whiteness of her face, nor the stunned horror in her eyes.

'It's not bad,' he insisted. 'Just a small patch. It's been there, quiescent, for a long time. That's why I was so tired. But there was no cough – and I was used to being tired, so I didn't pay much attention. I might have recovered from it without knowing I had it – if it hadn't flared up with the pneumonia.'

She spoke with effort. 'But . . . Bill . . . are they *sure* . . . it's T.B.?'

'Yes, darling. But it *isn't* serious, I promise you! Only – I'll have to go to a sanatorium for a few months – not more than six or eight I think. There's nothing to be frightened about.'

Sue could only look at him, speechless. She realized, dimly, that he was telling her the exact truth – that he would not insult her intelligence nor their relationship by lying to her. If he said it wasn't serious – it wasn't. If he said he would not be away more than six or eight months – then he wouldn't. She understood that, with the children, he could not be nursed at home. But Bill – with T.B.! Bill – going away from her!

She could think no further than this at the moment – but she needn't upset him with her reactions.

She sat motionless, looking out of the window, trying to keep her face blank while she got a grip on herself, to beat back the shock and force her mind into focus. It wasn't easy, but at last she stirred and looked at Bill with a faint grin.

'All right, Doctor,' she said.

4

Practical and definite

'You didn't stay long,' Kit said, glancing up from the papers on her desk.

'No, I didn't.' She crossed the room and dropped into a chair by the office window. 'He talked every single minute I was there – and he shouldn't. He knows better, too. Honestly! What makes men act so when they're sick?'

'You ought to know by this time. They're outraged by the whole thing.'

'No doubt. I wouldn't put it past them. Bill worries me to death. You know, I was frightfully upset when I discovered that the sanatorium where he's going only allows visitors once a month – but I can see why, now. If they let people in oftener the patients would talk themselves into a relapse every hour on the hour.' She stared gloomily out of the window and Kit returned to her papers.

There was a silence, broken presently by the eruption of four young student nurses on to the tennis court. Their shouts and laughter came in through the open window and Sue smiled briefly, remembering other student nurses on that court, in the days when she had been Director of Nurses there.

Her eyes wandered over the office with its cream-coloured walls, soft drapes, and mahogany desk; but she didn't envy Kit. The executive branch of nursing had never appealed to her as it did to Kit, though she had – she hoped – done fairly well with the job when she had it.

'Kitten,' she burst out suddenly, 'wouldn't you consider me able-bodied, healthy, and of average intelligence?'

Kit looked across the desk with a deliberately appraising eye. 'You're healthy, all right,' she admitted, 'and I don't suppose you're really feeble-minded, though I've sometimes won –'

'Oh, shut up!' said Sue, grinning. 'No, but listen, can you think of any good reason why, when Bill's away, I should lounge around at home living on the fat of his bank balance?'

'Well,' said Kit cautiously, 'It's supposed to be nice work if you can get it.'

'Not to me, it isn't. Not that Bill and I haven't done all right, but I don't want it *undone* now. There's the children's education coming up. There'll be Bill's expenses at the sanatorium. All right. Fine. But add the household expenses to that, plus the possibility that – that Bill's recovery ... may take longer than he thinks –'

'Well?'

'Yes – Well! Tell me one good reason why I shouldn't go back to work?'

'Hey! Are you arguing with me, or yourself, or Bill?'

'Bill, mostly, I suppose. I'm just trying it out on you first.'

'It sounds like good sense to me,' Kit said. 'What makes you think Bill would mind?'

'Because he's sick and not at all like himself. I'm afraid that if I pop up now worrying about finances he's going to feel badly. You know ... sort of helpless. I'm not *sure* he would, you understand – but he might, and I don't want that. He's taking it for granted that he's going to make the world's fastest recovery, he feels we're all provided for – so why worry about money?'

'Mm.' Kit's brown eyes were thoughtful and her long fingers played absently with a pencil on her desk. Then she laughed aloud. 'I have it,' she said. 'If you'll leave Bill to me I'll guarantee – absolutely – that by tomorrow he'll be begging you to get a job.'

Sue brightened, for when Kit looked like that things usually happened.

'How?' Sue demanded.

Kit shrugged. 'Well – after all – you poor little thing, sitting at home alone, brooding, unhappy. It's unhealthy, and bad for the children. You ought to have some kind of job.'

There was far more truth in this than Kit realized, all other considerations aside, and Sue's throat tightened. She swallowed and said lightly, 'Any time you want a recommendation, Mrs Machiavelli, just come to me!'

'It'll be a pleasure. Drop by tomorrow and get your working permit.'

'I'll do just that,' Sue rose.

'Wait a minute. Have you decided what you want to do?'

'Certainly. If Bill's willing I was coming around to see you tomorrow, with my hat in my hand, and say "Please, Madam, could you give a respectable, steady woman with good references a job as relief staff nurse in the new wing? I've heard tell you want one." '

Kit's eyes opened wide. 'Staff duty! *You?*'

'Just what,' Sue demanded with dignity, 'is the matter with *me?*'

'Nothing's the matter with you – except that you must be out of your mind. You were the first Director of Nurses here, you're the wife of the Chief of Staff – and you want to racket around on the floors. What's with you?'

'What's with me, in case it escaped your notice, is that I'm still a trained nurse, and I like *being* a trained nurse. Your job may have prestige, but it got on my nerves. I don't like spending my days beating my brains out over classes and affiliations. I like taking care of patients, and that's what I intend to do – if it's all right with you.'

'Naturally. After all, they're *your* feet. And it would be swell to have you, Sue. Goodness knows we need relief nurses. When did you want to start?'

'As soon as I can after Bill . . . goes. I'll have to let you know.' Sue moved towards the door. 'Thanks, Kitty.'

She drove home feeling almost lighthearted. The chance to do something practical and definite about the situation made all the difference, and she was no longer worried about Bill's reaction. Kit could be very serious and direct when she chose, and Bill respected her opinion. It *will* be good for me, too, Sue thought. In fact, it'll be a mercy.

As the car began its long climb up the mountain road Sue glanced out across the valley at the hospital, thinking how much it had changed and grown. When it was built, there had been only one doctor – Bill – with one intern to help him. Now there were a dozen staff doctors, an administrator, and interns all over the place – to say nothing of additions to the building itself.

It would be fun working in the new wing. Sue's eyes shone at the idea of being back in the thick of things once more, and her foot came down on the accelerator with so much vigour that the car leaped forward like a startled rabbit. It whirled into the little lane beside the house and came to so abrupt a stop that Bill, had he been there to see it, would have muttered about tyres for a week.

The thought of Bill was sobering, and Sue's brief elation vanished. She went quietly into the house, trailed by the children; she tickled the baby's toes, gave Veazie Ann a brief report on Bill's progress, and sat down to check over again the list of things he would need at the Indian Stream Sanatorium.

It was a small list – too small, Sue thought, yearning to load Bill with every known comfort. But after all, he would be on complete bed rest for some time and there wasn't much he could use. Anyway, the sanatorium was scarcely fifty miles away; she could always go over with more things if he needed them.

She rose and went out to the kitchen where she found Veazie Ann cleaning the pantry and talking to Baby Sue. The baby was kicking cheerfully in her bassinet just outside the pantry door while Tabitha and the twins grouped around her, earnestly singing, 'Twinkle, Twinkle, Little Star.'

'Mercy!' said Sue. 'It sounds like Grand Central Station! Veazie Ann, what did we do with Bill's suitcase – the pigskin?'

'It's up attic, but I dunno just where. I remember I wrapped it in somethin' to keep it nice. You goin' to pack?'

'I might as well. He's going day after tomorrow.' Sue's casual tone deceived the children, but not Veazie Ann, whose plump hands, busy among the shelves, faltered for an instant, though she made no comment.

'Mummy,' Tabitha demanded suddenly, '*why* does Daddy have to go to *another* hospital?'

'Because he needs some special care, darling. I explained all that . . . How would you kids like to come up in the attic with me?'

'Oh!' Tabitha clasped her hands. 'Can we dress up, Mummy? *Please!*'

'If you like."

Diverted, the children scampered after Sue up the broad front stairs, made a dash for the attic doorway, and clambered ahead of her into the crowded enchantment. They would make a fearful mess, but no matter.

Sue left them to their own devices while she looked for the pigskin bag, but even the children's excited voices, coming muffled from the depths of old trunks, could not stem the sudden wave of depression which swept over her. Why must this happen to Bill? And what was she to do without him? Her eyes filled and she plunged blindly into a closet under the eaves, struggling for self-control, and groping vaguely among the boxes and parcels stored there.

Her hand encountered a rectangular something wrapped in paper and she drew it out, hurriedly wiping her eyes on the back of her hand. The package was labelled 'Sue's white uniforms'.

Well – might as well look them over and see if they were all right. She hadn't given any thought, as yet, to the matter of uniforms.

She untied the string and, opening the cardboard box, shook out a uniform.

'Oops!' she said aloud.

'What, Mummy? What is it? What are you *doing*?' Tabitha stumbled across the floor, half in and half out of an old evening dress of Sue's. She stared at the uniform, for she had never seen her mother wearing any but the blue of the Visiting Nurse's. 'What's that?' she demanded.

'It's one of the uniforms I used to wear when I worked in Daddy's hospital – like Aunt Kit.' Sue was looking at the uniform in dismay. It had yellowed and the skirt was appallingly short.

'Put it on, Mummy! I want to see."

'So do I,' said Sue with emphasis. She slipped out of her dress and pulled the uniform on over her head. There were no studs in it, but she pulled it together at the waist, holding it with both hands. It lacked an inch and a half of meeting.

Tabitha gave a shriek of laughter.

'Oh, Mummy! You look silly! And it's too tight.'

'You'd better be thankful, young lady,' said Sue gravely, 'that's it's only a tiny bit too small.'

'Why?'

'Well, because –' said Sue helplessly, unable to explain to the seven-year-old Tabitha why, if the uniform must be too tight, it was gratifying to discover that one's figure had not changed *much*. Anyway, she'd have to buy new uniforms – and white shoes, too. She wondered where her school pin was, and scrabbled around in the box. She found it, presently, pinned on one of the uniforms, and tucked in a corner were several pairs of very yellow silk stockings.

Oh-oh! Sue thought. I'll need some white nylons, too. Goodness! I'd forgotten there were such things as silk stockings. And caps! I'll have to send for some, unless Kit has a couple to spare.

It wasn't until she had unearthed the pigskin bag and had gone downstairs with it – her mind still running on the various items needed to re-equip her as a staff nurse – that she made a discovery.

Her depression was gone – swamped as it had been earlier by the prospect of going back to work. She had not been deceiving Bill in the least; and Kit, the rat, must have known it all the time – for if ever a girl was desperately in need of distraction, change, and hard work, it was Sue Barton Barry.

5

Denham Two

THE breeze blowing in through the car window had a tangy coolness which did not quite belong with summer, even in the mountains, and the sky looked unusually blue and far away. Sue pulled her cape more closely around her and took a deep breath, pleasantly aware that she felt both cheerful and excited.

Good news from Bill was the backlog for her cheerfulness. He liked the sanatorium, did not mind the strict regime, and said that even in two weeks he had begun to improve. Added to this was the fact that she was going back to work.

Kit, who had had dinner at Sue's the night before, had been amused by Sue's frank satisfaction. 'I never saw anybody so nuts about nursing,' she said. 'Put a uniform on you and you're a gone goose. I don't get it – and I like nursing myself.'

'You've never been out of it. That makes all the difference. I don't know how to explain it, except to say that you miss it. You get homesick for it.'

'Could be,' Kit admitted, 'though I've never had a chance to find out. And anyway, what do you mean, you've been out of it? You've never entirely dropped your Public Health work.'

'That's not the same thing. There's nothing like staff work, really. It has everything.'

'It certainly has – if you like everything. I don't. In fact, I'll tell you a guilty secret that I've been carrying around with me for years. I loathe beds!'

'Beds?' said the astounded Sue.

'Yes, beds, and everything about them. I hate making them! I hate changing them! I hate tightening drawsheets! I've never gone close to a bed in my life that it hasn't snapped at my ankles or tried to fracture a kneecap. And I despise pillows – the perverse, squirming things, always mussed up and always crawling off somewhere!'

'Nonsense! Treat a pillow kindly and it'll do anything for you.'

'I don't want it to do anything for me except keep away from me! Let's not think about it. Did I tell you that you'll be working with Pat Glennon?'

'Who's she?'

'One of the best nurses we've got. She's relief nurse in charge of Denham Two, which is where you'll be working.'

'What's she like?'

'She's capable, for one thing. She's in her forties, snow-white hair, nice figure, very dark blue eyes – and a swell sense of humour. She was out of nursing for a while, raising a family, but her two kids are in college now, so back she came. Just another pillow juggler, like you.'

Sue grinned now, remembering this conversation, and glanced down at a small cardboard box on the seat beside her. The box contained a new crinoline cap, pleated and frilled and with a wide band of black velvet around it. Sue had not worn a cap since Tabitha was born and her glance at the box was affectionate.

The car bounced across the bridge over the Springdale River and turned up the winding mountain road on the other side, towards the high bluff on which the hospital stood.

The new wing had been completed two months before Baby Sue was born, and with its completion Bill had resigned as administrator to become the surgical Chief of Staff.

'I'm a surgeon,' he told Sue, 'and I intend to remain a surgeon. I can't do that and run a place that's mushrooming the way this one is. We need a trained administrator who is a good businessman.'

He had been happier ever since, Sue reflected as she parked the car near the hospital entrance and got out – gingerly – so as not to rumple her white uniform. She ran lightly up the hospital steps, paused briefly in the lobby to speak to Gertie, the telephone operator, and went on to the Nursing School Office.

A Supervisor who seemed too pretty to be anywhere but in Hollywood looked up as Sue came in, and sprang to her feet. 'Mrs Barry! How are you?' Then, as the telephone on her desk buzzed frantically, she said, 'Excuse me just a minute, please. Do sit down.'

Sue established herself on a chair beside a filing-cabinet and listened with amused interest to the one-sided conversation.

'Nursing School Office,' said the Supervisor crisply. 'Miss Arthur speaking ... Yes, I did, Miss Harmon ... No ... Well, you can't strip your floor of nurses like that, just because ... No, the time sheet has gone through. She'll just have to break her date.'

Miss Arthur hung up just as two student nurses came into the office.

'Miss Arthur,' the taller of the two began, 'I can't possibly relieve on Women's Surgical – anyway not after half-past five. I'm taking a train home at six.'

'Now wait a minute,' said Miss Arthur reasonably, 'you're on duty in the Operating Room until seven – so how can you take a train at six?'

'But we've finished operating,' the student wailed, 'and I've telephoned my mother, and –'

'And you're still on duty, and on call for the Operating Room. Women's Surgical is short of a nurse. Run along now and don't talk nonsense.' Miss Arthur grinned cheerfully, the student grinned sheepishly and departed with her friend, who remarked audibly just outside the door:

'I told you it wouldn't work, you dope!'

Sue and Miss Arthur exchanged amused glances.

'It takes a while to drum responsibility into some of them,' Miss Arthur said. 'How does it feel to be back, Mrs Barry?'

'Wonderful,' said Sue, 'and I promise not to ask to leave early no matter what time the trains run.'

'Oh! Well, naturally, Mrs Barry, if you – I mean –' she floundered for a moment and then said, 'Would you like to put your cap on here? The Nurses' Room in Denham will probably be crowded – it usually is when the shifts are changing. There's a mirror right behind you.'

While Sue put on her cap the Supervisor continued – apologetically – 'Miss Van Dyke has a class, so I'm to take you over to Denham and introduce you to Miss Patton, the floor Supervisor. And she – er – I mean – Miss Van Dyke told me to – to tell you not to boil any thermometers.' She laughed nervously and for a moment Sue was puzzled; then she understood. To the young Supervisor Sue was not just another staff nurse coming on duty; she was Dr Barry's wife; she was a former Director of Nurses; she was Miss Van Dyke's best friend.

Oh-oh! Sue thought. Oh *goodness*! And as she followed

Miss Arthur along the corridor which led to the new wing she felt a growing sense of panic. What if this attitude turned out to be general? What if the other nurses resented her? What if they assumed that she wouldn't do her share of the work — would, in fact, take advantage of her position? She had known of similar instances, equally unfair, in which a great deal of time and effort had been required before the matter was finally straightened out.

Oh, golly! Sue moaned to herself. Why didn't I think of this before? I wish I'd stayed at home and had a nervous breakdown in privacy!

Well, it was too late now. They were already approaching the glass-walled nurses' station on Denham, its overhead lights glaring down on white uniforms and caps.

A slim, dark-haired nurse with red harlequin glasses rose, and came to the door to meet them. The other nurses glanced up curiously and then went on with their charting.

Afterwards, Sue realized that the young Supervisor did not mean to say it — didn't, in fact, realize that she *had* said it — 'Miss Patton,' she began, 'this is your new relief nurse — Dr Barry's wife.'

Sue had a distinct, almost violent sensation of being unveiled; and at that moment, she felt, she would gladly have killed Miss Arthur. She had no chance to carry out any murderous intentions, for Miss Arthur added cheerfully, 'I know you'll be happy here, Mrs Barry,' and retreated down the corridor.

Miss Patton, however, was not very young, nor was she in the least disconcerted by this peculiar introduction. She smiled at Sue and said pleasantly, 'We're very glad to have you here, Mrs Barry. Won't you come into the Nurses' Room and leave your things, and then I'll show you around the floor.'

Her tone was formally friendly and it seemed to Sue that the blue eyes behind the harlequin frames were non-committal.

The Nurses' Room was cheerful with bright curtains and comfortable with armchairs but it was restless with the arrivals and departures of white-uniformed nurses. A row of lockers stood along one wall, and Miss Patton, after opening several, found an empty one. 'Take this,' she said, and then, after Sue had hung up her cape and put her cap box on the tiny shelf, 'Let's go, shall we? I'd like to show you around before I give the report.'

She sounded faintly harassed and Sue followed her at once.

The tour of the floor did not take long, because as Miss Patton explained, 'I realize that you know the floor routine and its general construction, so I'll just show you where things are kept.'

When they returned to the Nurses' Room, Sue met, for the first time, the nurse with whom she must work in close partnership day after day. They would be the only graduates on the floor except for private-duty nurses. They must share not only the work but the responsibility. They must learn one another's ways, habits, temperament, and points of view. They could be friends – or not.

Mrs Glennon was, as Kit had said, an attractive, white-haired woman in her forties and she greeted Sue cordially enough, and yet – was she or wasn't she a little guarded in her manner? Sue didn't know.

Peggy, the very young Nurses' Aide, was the only one who didn't leave Sue wondering. The girl was obviously too shy to care whether Sue were Dr Barry's wife or the kitchenmaid. There were, of course, other introductions as the nurses on the day shift appeared, but Sue didn't remember their names.

Then the relief shift sat down and the report began. Sue leaned forward listening intently, though she could not expect to remember much this first day, even though there were familiar Springdale names among the patients.

Mrs Glennon grinned at her sympathetically, and, when the report was finished, said kindly, 'It'll be half an hour before the day shift goes off. Why don't you look through the charts and get a little better idea of the patients?'

Sue was grateful for the suggestion, but it didn't work out as planned. There was too much going on in the office and every time Sue had worked her way half through a chart some other nurse wanted it. There seemed nothing for her to do except keep out of the way, and she envied Peggy, who was taking temperatures, and Eben, the orderly, who was busy answering bells.

The fifth chart had just been taken out of Sue's hands when Mrs Glennon appeared in the doorway.

'Finding it a little tough to concentrate?' she asked.

'Well,' said Sue ruefully, 'I'd probably do better if you just took me off somewhere and hung me on a hook.'

'Don't worry,' Pat Glennon said, 'everything will be simpler when these hyenas get off the floor.'

The day shift departed at last, with a great deal of chattering and laughter, and then the floor became startlingly quiet. Peggy came into the office and put down the temperature book.

'I'll tell you what,' Mrs Glennon said to Sue, 'if you'll chart the temperatures, I'll give the four o'clock medicines. You'll be medications nurse later on, but it hardly seems fair to dump it on you your first day.'

Sue felt almost childishly pleased at being given some-

thing to do and she attacked the charts with enthusiasm.
Peggy vanished and so did Mrs Glennon. There was a busy
silence of some minutes, and then Sue became aware that
a tall young man was standing in the office doorway. He
wore a bathrobe and regarded Sue with calm eyes.

'My name's Harvey,' he said. 'Tommy Harvey.'

Sue smiled at him. 'And I'm Mrs Barry,' she said. 'Can
I help you?'

'Well, I just thought somebody ought to know – Uncle
Billy's set his bed on fire.'

Sue sprang to her feet but the calm voice detained
her.

'It's all right, Mrs Barry. I put it out. I'm his room-mate.
And he didn't get burned. Eben's in there now.'

'Which room?'

'Twelve.' He broke off, for at that moment Eben, the
orderly, came out of a room two doors down, carrying a
loosely rolled bundle of bedclothes and surrounded by a
reek of burning wool. He was a big man, with grey hair,
and he looked capable, even if red with exasperation and
talking to himself.

'Pigheaded!' he was saying. 'Blithering idiot! Man his
age –'

His movement along the corridor fanned the smoulder-
ing bedclothes and as he passed the office doorway flames
burst from both ends of the bundle.

'Eben!' Sue cried. 'Look out!'

'I don't care what they say – he's away out in the left field.
He'd ought to be –' Eben continued tramping on, obliv-
ious.

'*Eben! You're on fire!*'

The urgency in Sue's voice got through this time and
Eben glanced down.

'Loddlemighty!' he yelled, and, leaping like a mountain goat, he fled towards the Utility Room, trailing smoke and flames. An instant later there was a loud hissing of water.

'Would you find Mrs Glennon and tell her?' Sue asked Tommy as she dashed past him to Room 12, where she found a white-haired Uncle Billy, very nonchalant in his stripped bed.

'What happened?' Sue asked him gently.

He turned his eyes towards her without turning his head.

'How should I know?' he asked, in a surprisingly deep voice. 'I was jest a-lying here and all at once Tommy commenced a-beating up on me.'

'Well – your bed was on fire,' said Sue reasonably.

'I ain't seen you before,' said Uncle Billy, evading the issue.

'I just came on duty here today. Are you all right? Hurt anywhere?'

'Sufferin' snakes! Here I be, so stiff with rheumatics I can't move hand nor foot! I ache in every mite of me! My joints is swole up like a pizened pup – and you wanta know if I –'

'I meant from the fire.'

'Of course I ain't hurt,' Uncle Billy roared, with an indignation which implied that he was made of asbestos.

Sue looked him over carefully, found no trace of any burns, and, taking a fresh sheet and blanket from his bureau drawer, remade his bed.

He eyed her in silence for a few minutes and then remarked suddenly, 'Ye're a nice girl. Pretty, too. I still like 'em pretty. So I'm a-going to tell ye sumpthing – *I ain't never going to smoke again long's I live!*'

'That,' Sue agreed, 'is a very sound idea.' She tucked him in and turned, to collide with Mrs Glennon.

'Tommy told me,' Mrs Glennon said. 'I've called the Supervisor and an intern. Is he all right?'

'He seems to be. I can't find any sign of burns.'

Mrs Glennon turned to Uncle Billy. 'What are we going to do with you?' she asked him, half-laughing, half-scolding. 'You just can't smoke in bed, Uncle Billy — unless Tommy is —'

'I've give it up,' said Uncle Billy firmly. 'You take them cigarettes and put 'em on the bureau where I can't reach 'em.'

They all laughed and then, as a Supervisor and a tall young intern appeared, Sue returned to her charts, where she made the most of three uninterrupted minutes before a woman appeared in the doorway. She was stout and middle-aged, and she carried a pair of enormous shoes, which she put on the desk.

'I'm Mrs Cutter,' she said. 'My husband came in this noon for some tests. He's been bleeding from his stomach. Will you hide these, please?'

'But —' Sue began.

'He won't stay. He's putting on his pants right now — but he can't go home without his shoes.'

'Oh-oh!' Sue rose and followed Mrs Cutter to a room at the far end of the corridor, where she found a large, pasty-faced man pacing the floor. His hair was tousled, his braces dangled, and he was talking to himself. As Sue appeared in the doorway he turned on her.

'You needn't think you can talk me out of it,' he shouted. 'I'm going home! There isn't a thing the matter with me. It's a lot of nonsense.' He turned, sweating, to his wife. 'Where's my shoes?' he demanded. 'I'm getting out of here.'

'Now, Jim,' Mrs Cutter quavered, 'I – I gave your shoes to the nurse. You can't –'

'Then I'll go without!' He yanked open the closet door and reached for his coat.

Sue spoke quietly from the doorway. 'Honestly, Mr Cutter,' she said, 'there's no need to be frightened. The tests aren't anything – and a stomach haemorrhage isn't necessarily serious.'

'Who's frightened?' he shouted.

'You are.'

He glared at her, speechless.

'But you needn't be,' Sue went on. 'If you have the tests done we'll know what the trouble is and can straighten it out. If you don't, you'll probably go on and on having trouble.'

He wavered visibly and then his panic returned. 'No! I'm going home right now!'

'By all means,' Sue told him so placidly that he stared at her again. 'Nobody wants to keep you here if you don't want to stay. But you have to be signed out, you know. I'll call your doctor right away.'

The prospect of facing an amused or stern doctor was not comforting and Mr Cutter's face fell. 'Oh!' he said. 'Er – well – I –'

Sue pulled up a chair. 'Do sit down a minute, Mr Cutter. All we want to do is make you as comfortable as we possibly can – and you don't look very comfortable right now. I'd like to tell you a little about those tests. I think you'll be pleasantly surprised.' She smiled at him so warmly that he smiled back in spite of himself and sat down.

'Now then' – Sue began her explanation, which was both simple and reassuring. When she had finished Mr Cutter grinned feebly.

'Women!' he said. 'All right. Have it your own way.' He turned to the relieved Mrs Cutter, who was standing quietly beside him, not having said a word in some minutes. 'Now, Millie, I want you to calm down. There's no use getting excited about these things.' He added to Sue, but kindly, 'My wife's a little hysterical.'

Sue exchanged a glance of complete understanding with Mrs Cutter, and managed to keep her face straight until she was outside in the corridor. She had just reached the office when one of the telephones rang. Sue picked up the receiver and said briskly, 'Denham Two – Mrs Barry speaking,' when the other telephone jangled at her. Meanwhile a masculine voice was saying in her ear, 'This is Dr Westman. I'd like to give you some orders on Mr Mullins.'

The other telephone rang again, louder this time, and Sue peered down the corridor. Neither Peggy, nor Mrs Weston, nor Eben was anywhere in sight.

'Yes, sir,' she replied into the first phone. 'Just a moment please.'

She reached for the second receiver, said 'Denham Two – Mrs Barry – just a moment please,' and went back to the doctor on the other line. 'Yes, sir, 200 milligrams of dicumarol. . . . Restrict fluids. . . . No, sir. Good-bye.' She hung up and turned to the second telephone.

The first one rang again.

A voice from the second announced, 'This is the Admitting Office. You're getting a patient of Dr Brownley's – Private Room 14 – gunshot wounds of shoulder. He's just gone up to the Operating Room.'

'Thank you,' said Sue through the prolonged ringing of the first telephone. She put back the second receiver and picked up the first. 'Denham Two – Mrs Barry. . . . No, she isn't. . . . Sorry.' She hung up.

Both telephones rang simultaneously.

With a despairing glance down the still empty corridors, Sue snatched up the two receivers, put one to each ear, and said 'Denham Two – Mrs Barry.'

Two voices spoke together, one demanding the ages and weights of three patients, the other giving orders from the Operating Room for the patient with the gunshot wound. One voice was pleasant, one was not. Sue dealt with each as rapidly as she could and had just finished when somebody behind her said:

'Having fun?'

Sue turned. 'Kitty! What on earth are *you* doing here?'

The telephones, miraculously, were silent.

Kit grinned. 'Well, my original plan was to call Denham Two-oo and go into the problem of Uncle Billy with Mrs Glennon – but the lines seemed to be busy.'

'*Seemed!*'

'Now! Now! You wanted to get back to fundamentals – and this is it.' Kit's startled eyes fell on Mr Cutter's shoes, which Sue had not had an opportunity to remove from the desk. 'What on earth? Aren't you getting a little *too* fundamental, maybe?'

'Oh,' said Sue lightly. 'You mean *those*? I thought they'd make the office look more homey. There's nothing like a man's shoes –' she broke off as Peggy and Mrs Glennon, drawn by some kind of hospital telepathy, appeared from opposite directions and converged on the office.

'I've got to report an admission and a lot of orders,' Sue told Kit. 'Do you mind if I tell Glennon right away – before you get started on Uncle Billy?'

'Go right ahead.'

Mrs Glennon greeted Kit cordially and with assurance, listened to Sue's account of the various telephone conver-

sations, and sent Peggy to make up an ether bed in Room
14.

'Shall I give Mr Mullins his dicumarol?' Sue asked.
'Miss Van Dyke wants to talk to you about Uncle Billy.'

'Oh! Thanks – if you would.' Pat Glennon's eyes were
twinkling at the mention of Uncle Billy and as Sue left the
office she thought, 'I'll say one thing for Glennon – nothing
bothers her.' It was a pleasant idea, for there is nothing
more difficult in staff duty than working with a nurse who
is always flustered.

Sue took Mr Mullins his dicumarol and found him a
charming old gentleman, but talkative. It was some minutes
before she could get away and when she returned to the
office Kit and Mrs Glennon were moving towards the
elevator, deep in discussion.

There were three lights on from the eight-bed ward and
Sue went to answer them. She had just taken a glass of
milk to the third patient when a wheeled stretcher rolled
down the corridor. Two nurses in operating gowns and
headpieces manipulated it skilfully into Room 14 and Sue
followed to help.

The unconscious figure on the stretcher was a boy of
perhaps nineteen, with curly blond hair and a very white
face. Sue, Peggy, and the two Operating Room nurses slid
him on to the warm bed. One of the nurses handed Sue
his chart.

'Poor kid,' she said. 'Didn't know the gun was loaded
and leaned on it. Luckily, the bullet missed the bone. It's
a clean wound so he'll be okay – up tomorrow probably.'
She backed out with the stretcher.

Sue left Peggy to watch the boy and was returning to the
office with the chart when she encountered Mrs Glennon,
coming from the elevator. Kit had vanished. Mrs Glennon

ran an expert eye over the chart Sue handed her, glanced up, and said, 'Oh, brother! Look what's coming!'

Sue looked, and saw, approaching the office, a man and a woman, both middle-aged. The man was tall and stooped, with greying hair and a receding chin. The woman was short – almost tiny – with violently hennaed hair, a hard face, and very expensive clothes. A half-dozen necklaces dangled around her neck; her hands glittered with rings and her wrists with bracelets. She paused before Sue and Mrs Glennon, looked them up and down, and said with harsh determination:

'My son has just come from the Operating Room, and I want special nurses *at once*.'

Pat Glennon said pleasantly, 'We'll try to get them for you. I'll call Nursing School Office right away.'

'Oh?' said the woman contemptuously. 'I suppose that means that if I have enough pull I can get nurses, and if I haven't – I can't. Is that it?'

Pat Glennon's tone was quiet. 'Our registry is not run that way,' she said. 'If special nurses are available, you will get them; if they aren't, I'm afraid there's nothing you can do except wait.'

The woman looked at her platinum-and-diamond wrist watch, said, 'Very well. We'll see. Will you show me to my boy's room, please. Come, Alfred.'

Sue went with them, showed them in, gave Peggy a glance of warning, and was about to leave when the woman said sharply, 'What's that water doing here?'

'That water' was a fresh pitcherful which Peggy had brought a few minutes before, and had put on the bedside table.

'Your son may have water – when he is awake enough,' Sue explained. 'Just sips at first, but later –'

She was interrupted by the harsh voice. 'Are you *sure*,' it said, 'that is *fresh* water – and not some left over from another patient?'

'I just brought it myself, this minute,' Peggy said, tartly, her shyness overcome by outrage.

Sue backed hastily out of the room.

'Wow!' she said to Pat Glennon in the office, 'I hope you were able to get specials.'

'I got one for this shift anyway. She'll be here in half an hour.'

'Thank heaven! That woman really is Something!'

'Oh, she'll be all right,' Pat Glennon said serenely. 'She's just shocked and upset and afraid her boy won't get good care, but she'll see in a day or so, and then she'll calm down. They always do.'

In the next hour and a half, Sue changed three beds, went to first supper, helped carry the trays, persuaded a delirious man that the room across the hall was not the kitchen in his own house and spent a maddening fifteen minutes struggling with the filter in a transfusion set.

Mrs Glennon, meanwhile, was working on charts, giving medicines, attending to ringing telephones and to doctors who strolled into the office and claimed her immediate attention.

Then there was a lull, in which Sue was thankful to sit down in the Nurses' Room, and rest her tired feet.

The visitors came at seven. They came in hordes. They swarmed in the corridor, peered into rooms, chattered, laughed, or wept. Sue, who by this time was cleaning syringes, in one of the Utility Rooms, was interrupted again and again by alarmed women who spied her red head against the white-tiled walls and dashed in to tell her that father, husband, or brother was in agony from a headache,

a stomach-ache, or a funny kind of pain in his back –
and nothing had been done for him. It was always, Sue
noticed, during visiting hours that the convalescent patients
developed these symptoms, for none of them had com-
plained at supper-time.

Other visitors came asking for cracked ice, more chairs,
dishes for ice-cream, vases for flowers, knives to cut cakes
or pies, and innumerable other small requests whose object
was to cheer the sick.

Sue reassured, explained, brought dishes, arranged
flowers, and disposed of boxes, paper bags, and string. So
did Peggy and Eben.

Sue's feet pounded on the linoleum and her head was
beginning to ache – though she scarcely noticed it, for she
was enjoying herself.

The visitors left at last, and then a new round began.
There were more temperatures to chart, more dressings to
do, tired backs to rub, beds to straighten, blankets to dis-
tribute, icecaps and hot water bags to fill, side rails to put
up.

The four members of Denham's relief staff passed and
repassed one another with companionable grins and occasional pauses to exchange incidents. Eben was splutter-
ing because Uncle Billy had insisted that there was a fish in
his drinking water. Peggy was enchanted to report that
meek little Mr Dawson was in very high spirits, the result
of having come off victor in a quarrel with his large dom-
ineering wife during visiting hour. Pat Glennon emerged
from Room 3 shaking with laughter, to announce that Mr
Flaherty, a new patient of that morning did not want his
back rubbed because 'it had been rubbed for fourteen years
and was the cause of all his trouble'.

At nine o'clock the overhead lights in the corridor were

put out and the only illumination came from the open doorways of rooms and from dimmed bulbs set into the corridor walls, so that the relief staff became hurrying white ghosts. The office, in contrast, was a blaze of fluorescent light which turned faces yellow and lipstick blue.

'How are you doing?' Pat Glennon asked Sue, encountering her in the kitchen.

'To tell the truth, I'm having fun. And my patients are all settled for the night. What's next?'

Mrs Glennon looked at her watch. 'Oops! It's twenty-five to eleven. So -- we count narcotics, make a final inspection, and then you go home. I stay on to give the report to the night nurse.'

When the narcotics had been counted, checked, re-checked and the book signed, Sue pushed back her desk chair and stood up gingerly on hot feet.

'Tired?' Pat Glennon asked her.

Sue nodded. 'All the same,' she said, 'there's nothing like staff work. It's like coming home again.'

'I know exactly what you mean. That's the way I feel, too.'

They smiled at one another in a new and pleasant comradeship. Then Pat Glennon said with complete sincerity:

'Wasn't it lucky we had such an easy night?'

6

'A nice boy and a good doctor, but—'

'Oh, Veazie Ann,' Sue cried, sitting up in bed. 'You shouldn't!' Her face was flushed, her hair was tousled, and one curling red lock dangled crazily over her right eyebrow.

'Fiddlesticks!' Veazie Ann set the breakfast tray down on Sue's bedside table. 'Ye been a-goin' it fit to run under for a week now – both to home and to the hospital. Now it's your time off ye better relax a mite. Sakes! Them young ones made a regular rats' nest of the bed!'

'It was Jerry. Tabitha and Johnny are reasonable snugglers, but Jerry really puts his back into it. I'm probably black-and-blue all over.' Sue yawned and stretched. Then she sprang out of bed. 'One second while I brush my teeth.' She vanished into the bathroom.

Veazie Ann straightened the covers with a maternal hand, turned them back, and stood waiting until Sue returned.

'There now! I want ye should eat every mite.' She settled the tray on Sue's lap.

'Wow!' said Sue happily, looking at the pile of hot buttered toast, the gold and white of eggs in a nest of bacon, the steaming silver pot of coffee, the huge glass of orange juice. 'You want me to be known as Mrs Wayaton?'

' 'Twouldn't hurt. I'll bet ye've lost five pounds this

week.' Veazie Ann sat down in an armchair by the open window, smiling at the sound of the children's voices from the lawn.

Sue was attacking her breakfast with appetite, but she avoided looking at the empty twin bed beside her own – a fact which was not missed by Veazie Ann, who considered the matter and then asked casually:

'Why don't ye have Kit over this evening?'

'Well – no. I'd sort of like to be with the children, and go to bed early.' She took an enormous bite of toast, waited until she had swallowed it, and then added: 'I want to get used to leading two lives.'

'What *do* ye mean?'

'I mean that coming into this quiet house, at night, after the hospital, is kind of a shock after you've been in high gear for eight hours. You come steaming in – and everybody is asleep, and nobody wants anything, and I don't have to *do* anything. I run around in circles for an hour after I get home.'

'Hm. Want I should wait up for ye?'

'Mercy, no! I'll adjust.'

'Well, ye're a sight better off like that than if you was just a-settin' around home all the time.'

'Certainly. But I'd still like to have these two days here by myself, with just you and the children.'

'Just's you say, child. . . . What happened last night?'

A dimple appeared at the corner of Sue's mouth. 'So that's it! You, Too, Can Feel Awful. Life Can Be Terrible – tune in at this station on Friday, at ten A.M., for the next dismal instalment.'

'Hoighty-toighty!' said Veazie Ann comfortably. 'Well, what did?'

'Plenty. The place was a madhouse. Jim Prouty – you

know, he's Ira's cousin who has pneumonia — got out of bed and wandered into Mr Gerry's room — scared the poor man to death. Oh, and I must tell you — one of the admissions was a huge, burly man about forty; he's a summer visitor — came in with a ruptured disc — that's an injury to the spine. I got him settled in bed, and I noticed that he seemed pretty wild-eyed and full of loud talk, and he kept looking at the patient next to him, who was having a transfusion —'

'I should think he might!' Veazie Ann said, round-eyed. 'All them contraptions, an' fillin' folkses' arms full of blood!'

'Yes, I know; but still — anyway, the transfusion filter got plugged, so I went in to change it, and the new man kept saying that nobody seemed to know what they were doing around here. I realized that he was scared, but I thought the other men in with him could calm him down better than I could, so I didn't say anything.' She paused to dunk her toast in her coffee.

'Do go on, Sue!'

'Well, the next thing I knew, Gertie called up and asked if we'd lost a patient. Pat Glennon said of course not, but Gertie said that a big man had come tearing out of the elevator and through the lobby, and when they tried to stop him he ran like the dickens. So Ann and I went down to the eight-bed ward, and sure enough — no ruptured disc! They said he got into his clothes in one minute flat and just went.'

'Why didn't some of them other fellers let ye know?'

'That's what I wanted to know. They sort of stammered around but I guess they felt it was his business. So that was that — except that Uncle Billy fell out of bed, and his language was something to hear. I was perfectly fascinated.

Kit is trying to get him sent to a convalescent home. The hospital isn't any place for him, really. He's not going to get any better.'

'Land of Liberty, Sue! I don't wonder ye feel like you was in a pressure cooker.'

Sue laughed and fell silent, her mouth full of bacon and eggs.

'Didn't ye tell me one of them student nurses was named Macgraw?' Veazie Ann demanded suddenly.

'That's right. Marian Macgraw.'

'Hm. Mattie Dickson's daughter married a Macgraw from over Lebanon way.'

'I know. It's the same. The kid came over to my table in the Dining Room the other night and told me rather shyly, that she'd heard a lot about me because her grandmother lived in Springdale and was always talking about the time she broke her hip, and about the Visiting Nurse, Sue Barton, who took care of her. Said her grandmother had pointed me out once, in the village, so she felt she knew me.'

'Mattie and me went to school together. Seems funny to think she's got a granddaughter old enough to be a nurse. Land! How time flies! What's the child like?'

'She's a nice youngster,' said Sue warmly. 'A little on the plump side, with a round face – not pretty but pleasant-looking. As a matter of fact, I've been rather worried about her.'

'How come?'

'Well, she's just back from her vacation, and the first two days she was on the floor she was very cheerful and happy, and then, all of a sudden, she stopped being. Of course, I've only seen her from two-thirty to three-thirty, but I noticed that much. She doesn't laugh any more, and she stays off by herself. Seems to be brooding. I don't know what's happened, and neither does Mrs Glennon – but something has.'

'Likely, it's just a spell. Young ones that age git spells.' Veazie Ann pulled herself out of the chair and came to take the tray. 'Now you jest rest there, Sue. I'll keep the children downstairs. And you forgit about that hospital for a while.'

When Veazie Ann had gone Sue curled down among the pillows intending to drowse, and failed. So she got up and prepared to enjoy her time off.

She did enjoy it, up to a point, but only because of the children, for at every turn she came up against the bleakness of Bill's absence – his tools, his fishing tackle, a tobacco pouch, an old battered felt hat which dropped at her feet when she was looking for Tabitha's Mackinaw on the back porch. And the two evenings were bad, despite Veazie Ann's efforts to distract her.

When her off-duty time was over Sue went back to the hospital thankfully. The pressure of work relaxed her, and the bright, glass-walled fluorescence of the office surrounded her with security; she would not find any battered felt hats there. She trundled happily around with the dressing cart enjoying the easy comradeship of the staff, hummed under her breath as she gave out the medicines, and listened with an unexpected upsurge of sympathy to other people's troubles.

She still worried occasionally about the nurses' attitude towards her – if they had an attitude. She wasn't sure, for everyone was pleasant enough, and she never felt left out, but the nurses did seem guarded in their conversation, and there was a surprising lack of normal hospital gossip in the Nurses' Room – at least, when Sue was there.

Tonight, however, she didn't care. She was too thankful to be back at work.

Peggy was off, and, although Sue missed the child's quiet helpfulness, she was interested in Margot Harrison, the student from the day shift who was taking Peggy's place.

Margot Harrison was newly a senior, a trim attractive girl with a wide pleasant mouth and smooth brown hair which shone beneath the wings of her cap. Her composure of manner was so unusual for her age that Sue commented on it to Pat Glennon while they were checking off medicine in the office.

'She's a darned nice kid,' Pat Glennon said, 'and she's going to make a sweet nurse. The patients are crazy about her, and if you'll notice you'll find that she does a terrific amount of work without ever seeming to hurry – though goodness knows, I wouldn't blame her today if she didn't do a thing.'

'Why?' Sue asked, reaching for another chart.

'Today's her birthday and she's supposed to be off. What's worse, there's going to be a party for her at home this evening – and she won't be there. Somebody fouled up the time sheet, and Patton had to put her on relief.'

'Oh, no! The poor kid!'

'Exactly. I know darned well she's horribly disappointed but there hasn't been a squeak out of her – no sulks – no self-pity. She's just going along about her business as if nothing had happened –' She broke off as Margot Harrison appeared in the office doorway with twinkling eyes.

'Well,' she announced, and there was laughter in her voice, 'now I've seen everything.'

'*What?*' Sue and Pat demanded together – not without apprehension.

'Somebody,' Margot said, 'has given Uncle Billy *half* of a cake.'

'And –?'

'And – it's got thick chocolate icing on it – or it had – but the icing is on Uncle Billy now – even his eyebrows and hair – and on the bedclothes. The cake part is mostly in the bed. In fact, he's sitting on a good deal of it.'

'Oh, mercy!' Pat Glennon moaned.

'Don't worry, Mrs Glennon. I'll fix him up right away. It's just that he's having such a good time that I –' she broke off as a light flashed on the indicator board over the desk. 'Oops!' she said. 'There goes Mr Sanderson. He wants to be turned again.'

'But I just turned him,' Sue protested.

'I know, but he gets sort of frantic because he can't move. It must be awful, really, if you're the nervous kind.' She was gone with the words in a flutter of blue and white.

'See what I mean?' Mrs Glennon said.

'I certainly –'

The telephone rang.

Pat Glennon answered it, scribbled some notes on the back of an X-ray requisition, and turned to Sue.

'Would you mind finding Eben for me, Mrs Barry? There's an emergency admission coming: accident case with internal injuries, hit-and-run driver – and an abdominal prep to be done right away.'

Sue finally located Eben in the eight-bed ward, and broke the news to him. On the way back to the office she encountered Margot Harrison, her arms full of sheets and towels.

Sue paused to announce the emergency case, since admitting a patient to the floor was usually a student's job. Then she glanced inquiringly at the sheets and towels. 'Uncle Billy?' she asked.

'Well, yes – I didn't want him to grind any more crumbs than necessary into his back – but I guess he'll have to wait if there's an emergency coming. I don't suppose it'll do him any harm, really, will it?'

'No, it won't,' Sue agreed. 'And after all, it isn't every day he gets a chance to roll in a cake.' She paused, and then asked suddenly, 'How old are you?'

'*Almost* twenty.'

Sue smiled.

'You're a good nurse – did you know that?'

The girl flushed. 'That's an awfully nice thing to say, Mrs Barry, and it means a lot, coming from you.'

It was Sue's turn to flush, but before she could reply, Margot went on, 'All the kids know about you, Mrs Barry, and what a swell nurse you are. I . . . wanted to say . . . we're terribly sorry about Dr Barry. He's so nice and we learned such a lot, working with him in the O.R. You know, he did the first operation I ever saw.'

'He did the first operation *I* ever saw, too.'

Margot's eyes were suddenly round. '*No kidding!*' she said.

Sue laughed. 'He was an intern in my hospital when I was in training.'

'He – he *was*? I mean – you *were*? How perfectly swell! I wish, sometime, you'd –'

She was interrupted by the ghostly, amplified voice of the communications system.

Dr Warren! it said. *Dr Frank Warren!*

Margot Harrison's face was suddenly red. 'I'd better dump this stuff in Uncle Billy's room,' she said hastily, and went on down the corridor.

The amused and interested Sue returned to the office just as a gangling, pleasant-faced intern approached it from the direction of the X-ray Rooms. He grinned at Sue, chucked Pat Glennon under the chin, and picked up the nearest telephone.

'Dr Warren speaking,' he said. 'Yes, Dr Mackin. No, I won't let him get away. Yes, sir. I'll see that the operative permit is signed. No, sir – I'll attend to it personally. Right!' He hung up and turned. 'Hiya, baby,' he said to Margot Harrison, who had reappeared during the telephone conversation and now moved around him to tear a blank sheet of paper from a scratch pad, though she did nothing with it, once it was torn off.

'Hi,' she returned casually – too casually, Sue thought.

Dr Warren pulled out a desk chair and sat down, his long legs sprawled before him, and addressed himself to Sue and Mrs Glennon.

'Papa Mackin's upset,' he said. 'He's been called to operate on your admission, and he's afraid everybody won't do everything just right.'

The girls laughed, for Dr Mackin, though an excellent surgeon, was notoriously fussy, and given to fuming, worrying, and tantrums.

'Are you scrubbing with him, Frank?' Mrs Glennon asked.

'Yup.' Dr Warren stood up, stretched bone-crackingly, gave his head a shake, said 'Wow, but I'm tired,' and automatically picked up the receiver as the telephone rang again.

'Yes? This *is* Dr Warren. You sure it's a real haemorrhage? Oh-oh! I'll be right up – but look, baby, I'm due in the O.R. in just a few minutes – emergency operation – so you'd better get hold of Bob Jassey, too, because, deeply as it grieves me, I can't stay with you long. Okay. 'Bye.' The receiver clanked into its cradle.

He gave the belt to his white trousers a hitch, grinned at the girls again, changed the grin to a fairly recognizable attempt at a leer, said, 'Remind me to come back to you, sweethearts,' and was gone, leaving Sue and Pat laughing and Margot Harrison half-smiling.

Poor kid, Sue thought. Must they *always* get crushes on the interns? The old saying about people who live in glass houses came back to her suddenly – but after all, she had never had any flash-in-the-pan crush on Bill – she had scarcely realized how she felt about him until the night of her graduation.

It was at this point that a nurse from the Emergency Room swung a noiseless stretcher out of the elevator. On it lay a man in his early thirties with a week's growth of stubble almost hiding his waxen face. His eyes were closed and he was breathing stertorously. A miasma of whisky hung over the stretcher.

'Alcoholic?' Pat Glennon asked the Emergency Room nurse as they slid the stretcher into an empty room.

'No. Just a lumberjack on a spree.'

'Is he unconscious from drink or the accident?'

'Both, I guess. You ought to see his father, though! The old man must be over seventy, and drunk as a skunk. Seems he's cook in the same lumber camp as his son. The food must be dandy. Anyway, they both came out together to have a good time. You don't want him off the stretcher, do you?'

'No. He'll be going right up as soon as he's prepped.'

'Okay – but *please* send the stretcher back to us afterwards. Here's your chart.' She handed it to Margot Harrison, who was nearest, and hurried away.

The patient was all ready to go to the Operating Room

when Margot Harrison dashed into the office with the chart, all her composure gone.

'Oh, Mrs Glennon!' she exclaimed. 'The operating permit isn't signed!'

'Mercy!' Pat said, exasperated. 'I thought Frank Warren was going to attend to it personally. Well, I might have known! Honestly! These interns!'

She picked up the telephone and called the Admitting Office.

There was a flurry of conversation and two more calls before she finally hung up.

'Well,' she said, 'they let the father get away, but one of the State Troopers was still around. He's gone after the old man, and all we can do is wait. The O.R. will have a fit, of course, but there isn't anything else we can do.'

'Why didn't the Admitting Office do it?' Sue inquired.

Pat sighed. 'Because there's a volunteer on duty there tonight, and she doesn't know anything about anything. I'd better go and have a look at him.' She left the office, calling back over her shoulder to Sue, 'Stall off the O.R. if they call, will you?'

Sue glanced at Margot Harrison, who was gloomily holding the patient's chart. 'What's the matter?' Sue asked.

'Well, I just don't think it's fair to blame Frank. He was called upstairs from here. He didn't have a chance to attend to it. And he was terribly tired. You can't wonder if he forgot it. And anyway, why did old Mackin have to dump it on Frank? The Admitting Office should have done it – or we should.' She paused for breath.

'But look,' said Sue reasonably, 'the operating surgeon, himself, can always sign it, and take the responsibility, so why all the dither?'

'Because he told Frank to do it – and Frank promised. Now, if there's a slip-up, Mackin will just take Frank apart!'

'I see,' said Sue. 'Anyway, you can stop worrying. Here comes your signer. He can't have gone very far.'

A State Trooper was approaching with a firm grip on the arm of a reeling, dirty, dishevelled, and very lively old man. They halted in the doorway and the old man grinned at Sue and Margot, baring long, tobacco-stained teeth.

'Wash want, girls?' he demanded.

The State Trooper answered. 'I told you before, Mr Batters. They want you to sign a paper giving permission for your son to be operated on.'

'Paper?' The old man was suddenly suspicious. 'Me, I ain't gonna sign nothin'. Tricks.' He lurched and caught at the door casing.

'Better sit him down,' Sue told the Trooper, and together they eased the swaying figure on to one of the office chairs, where he peered around, trying to focus his eyes.

'Where'sh Charlie?' he demanded. 'I losht Charlie. He gone 'n' left me?'

'No,' Sue told him gently. 'He was hurt by a car. Don't you remember? And won't you please sign this?'

He pushed aside the chart she put before him. 'No! Wun't!' He obviously had no idea where he was and no realization of the accident.

Eben appeared in the doorway. 'Mrs Glennon,' he said, 'wants to know how you're coming.'

'Slow but sure –' Sue was beginning and was interrupted by Mr Batters, who was peering at Eben.

'What'sh he want? Fight?'

Sue stepped forward, her patience exhausted, and said firmly, 'Mr Batters, do you want to sit here all night?'

'Sure. Pretty girls. Nice place. We c'n have party.'

'No party,' said Sue quietly. 'This is for Charlie. Charlie wants you to sign it.'

'Does, eh?' He blinked once or twice and then said slowly, 'Okey-doke. Gimme it.'

Sue laid the permit before him and handed him a pen. He took it obediently, grinned, burst into a howl of laughter and announced proudly:

'Joke's on you, girlie. Can't read – *or* write!'

The State Trooper galvanized suddenly. 'Mark a cross on that line, Pop, and do it now – or I'll throw you in the jug.'

'Right here!' Sue placed a finger on the line.

The old man looked from Sue's face to the Trooper's. Then, very uncertainly, he reached out and traced a shaky cross on the paper below Sue's finger.

'That's all, Pop. Come on.' The Trooper hoisted him to his feet and they wavered out of the office, followed by Sue's thanks.

'Now then,' said Sue briskly, 'Mrs Glennon and I will sign it as witnesses, but Dr Warren has to make a note on it saying that the old man can't write – and sign *his* name on –' she broke off as the telephone rang.

It was the Operating Room, demanding irritably to have the patient Batters sent up at once, and stating ominously that Dr Mackin was in.

'The patient will be up in a minute,' Sue assured the voice. 'Is Dr Warren there?'

Dr Warren was not there. He was on the third floor, but due in the O.R. immediately.

Sue called the third floor, and was informed that Dr Warren couldn't come to the telephone at the moment, and was there any message?

'No, thank you,' said Sue wearily, and went down the corridor to consult Pat Glennon, with Margot Harrison close on her heels. She found Mrs Glennon beside the stretcher, her fingers on the patient's pulse. Eben leaned against the wall, waiting.

'Well,' Mrs Glennon said, when Sue had explained, 'we'll just have to send him up, Frank or no Frank. He can check on the permit there, before he scrubs.'

'But Mrs Glennon – Dr Mackin's in!' Margot pointed out suddenly.

'So what?'

'Ah – ah – look, *please*, Mrs Glennon, couldn't I just run up to the third with the chart, and have Frank – I mean – well, you know how Mackin is. Frank will have an awful time with him if he finds out about all this.'

'Frank'll survive it,' said Pat dryly. Then, glancing at the girl's face, 'Oh! All right, kid. Skip along if you want to.'

'Oh, thank you! I'll meet Eben at the elevator upstairs – with the chart.' Margot fled.

Pat Glennon grinned at Sue but her only comment was, 'Lordy, am I glad I'm not young!' She looked down at the unconscious Charlie. 'His pulse is a lot better than it was. You may as well start along, Eben – but look around for Miss Harrison when you get out of the elevator.'

'Yes, ma'am,' said Eben.

The floor returned to normal and Sue was dumping an armful of soiled towels into the laundry bag when Margot came back, panting but triumphant. She caught a glimpse of Sue's white uniform in the Utility Room and paused.

'What a rat-race!' she said. 'Frank had *just* left when I reached the third floor, so I *ran* all the way up – three more flights – and caught him right by the O.R. elevator!

He almost dropped dead when he saw that permit. But everything is all right now.'

Sue put a clean cover over the laundry hamper.

'Did you tell Dr Warren what we went through straightening out his mess?'

'Oh, *no*! I mean, there wasn't time – and anyway –'

'Never mind,' said Sue smiling, but with the sudden resolve that young Dr Warren was, nevertheless, going to hear *all* about it.

The opportunity came sooner than she expected.

Twilight was beginning and Pat Glennon's voice carried down the corridor to Mr Sanderson's room, where Sue had just finished turning him again.

'Goodness!' the voice said. 'It's time, already, to put on the lights. Harrison, would you run upstairs to the I.V. Room and get this saline and glucose?'

'Yes, Mrs Glennon.' Margot's even steps receded in the direction of the stairway.

A moment later there was a rattle of elevator doors opening and closing, followed by the consequential pat of rubber-soled shoes on linoleum. Sue placed Mr Sanderson's water pitcher nearer to his hand and then, having normal curiosity, stepped out into the corridor. 'Charlie' had come back, accompanied by Dr Warren, an Operating Room nurse, and a blood transfusion. Poor Charlie was a motionless, foreshortened lump on the stretcher, but as the procession moved down the corridor Pat Glennon switched on the lights and Sue noted that his colour was good, and that neither Dr Warren nor the nurse had the tense look which means a patient is in poor condition.

Eben and Pat Glennon appeared suddenly and among them they got Charlie into bed. Then, as Pat remained to check the transfusion flow, Sue followed Dr Warren to the office, where he was already settled at the desk to write up his notes.

'Was it a bad job?' she asked.

'Nope, chipped pelvis and shock. He'll be up and around in a few days. But Brother, was Mackin in a lousy humour!'

'That must have been fun! It was lucky Margot Harrison got that permit up to you in time.'

'Sure was,' he agreed absently. 'Harrison's a sweet kid.'

'You don't know the half of it,' Sue told him firmly.

He swung around in his chair, his pleasant young face suddenly concerned. 'Why? Did she get into any trouble about it?'

Sue laughed. 'Not exactly, but things were spinning around here for a while. Harrison ought to win, hands down, as a marathon runner; but, as she said, Dr Mackin wasn't going to tear you limb from limb if she could prevent it.'

The boy's face softened. 'No kidding! Did Harrison say that?'

'She did, when the permit came up unsigned. Do you want to hear our lurid tale?'

'Yes,' he said. 'I most certainly do.'

'All right.' Sue leaned back against the tiny office washbowl and told him the entire story.

'I'm terribly sorry,' he said. 'Honestly. And Margot didn't need to run herself into a coronary. I could have taken what was coming to me. But it *was* swell of her! I – Where the heck is she, anyway?'

'Probably on her way down from the I.V. Room,' Pat Glennon said from the doorway behind him.

'Thanks. I – I – Well, thanks!'

He swung out of the office just as the stairway door opened and Margot Harrison emerged, a large, glass flask of saline and glucose in each hand. The light from the office shone clearly upon her, and upon the gangling figure of Dr Warren. She regarded them with a benign smile.

The tall figure of the intern covered the few steps to the stairway door almost before it closed. He halted squarely in Margot's way. Then, as she stopped, and looked up, surprised by his purposeful manner, he took the two flasks from her hands, set them on the floor, picked her up by the elbows as if she were a child, kissed her soundly, put her down again, replaced the flasks in her hands and said, 'How's about a date with me?'

Sue beamed. Pat Glennon grinned for a moment, and then said, under her breath, 'Not so good – maybe.'

'Why?' asked Sue.

'Well – Frank's a nice boy, and he's a good doctor, but when it comes to girls, he plays the field.'

'Oh! That's too bad, because Harrison doesn't fit into that picture, I think.'

'No, she doesn't, and I'd hate to see the kid get hurt.' She paused, glanced at the corridor clock, and added, 'Young love or no love, we've got a busy night ahead of us. You'd better go to first supper, Sue, because I doubt if Harrison can eat at this point.'

Sue laughed and went, pleased and relieved because, at last, Pat Glennon had called her 'Sue'.

7

Day off

THE uproar customary to the Barry household at 8.15 on a school morning was in full swing.

'Mummy! He's got my blue jersey and *I* want to wear it!'

'Mummy, you forgot my lunch money yesterday. Miss Rivers told me to remind you, only I forgot. I *have* to have lunch money!'

'Mummy! Do I *have* to finish my milk?'

'Mummy! Is that the bus?'

Sue covered her ears wondering how nurses with children, but without a Veazie Ann, ever managed. Maybe they didn't. Maybe they just went quietly crazy.

'*Children!* Let me hear myself think! Here's your lunch money, Tabs, in this envelope. Boys — no, it's too late to change jerseys! Finish your milk, Johnny — and then all of you scamper.'

They left at last, with shouts, with trampling, with desperate returns for another hug, erupting through the front door toward the orange bus winding slowly up the hillside. Their departure left the house so suddenly and oppressively still that it awoke Baby Sue, who had been sleeping placidly in her basket throughout the commotion.

'Ahg,' she said experimentally.

Sue laughed and picked her up. 'You can't be hungry,' she said, her lips against the soft down on the baby's head. 'You've just had breakfast.'

'Likely she's a-thinkin' about her bath,' Veazie Ann said, giving the sink a final wipe. 'I'll tend to her, Sue. You go git fixed up. Ye want to be real glorified-lookin' for Bill.'

'There's plenty of time. Visiting hours don't begin until two, and I'm only going to wash my hair.'

'Best do it now and git it over, so's it'll be set good. And ye ought to make an early start, so's not to have to hurry. Them roads over there be a-weary of life an' afflicted.'

'That's putting it mildly – but I'll be careful.'

'Ye better. What ye goin' to wear?'

'That new honey-coloured dress.'

'Good. Ye'll look real peart an' sassy. It'll tickle Bill.'

Sue had hoped that it would; and now, further encouraged, she took extra pains with her hair and her nails, and dressed carefully. Bill, she thought gratefully, was not the kind of husband who never knew what you had on. He always noticed.

She drove sedately out of the yard, but her promise to be careful on the 'afflicted' roads was not easy to keep. The fifty miles to Indian Stream Sanatorium seemed endless and despite good intentions her pressure on the accelerator gradually increased until, at last, she shot through the sanatorium gateway in a spurt of gravel, sped past lawns and shrubbery, and parked with an unaccustomed jerk.

Once inside, she made a definite effort and accepted with very good grace the untangling of red tape which lay between visitor and patient. But she almost ran down a long corridor to the door marked 406.

'*Bill!*'

The face on the pillow turned quickly and she saw the bright, familiar grin.

'Hi!' They exclaimed together, laughed, and began all over again, but for the first few minutes they only babbled

foolishly, and it was some time before Sue could settle
herself and appraise Bill calmly.

Then she realized that his colour was normal, and the
bones in his face were covered with a healthy layer of
flesh.

'You've gained!' she said.

'Darned right, I have. My lesion's healing nicely, too.
I've seen the plates. And I'm getting. . . .' He described his
treatment in detail and with approval.

'Oh, Bill, that's wonderful! I'm so glad! And you like
it here.' It was a statement, not a question.

'*Like* it!' said Bill outraged. 'I'm going nuts! Let me out
of this and I hope I never see a bed again, even in the
distance. And am I sick of that window!'

'But it's a nice view, and the boxwood is so lovely –'

'Oh, sure. The boxwood is great. Once a week a man
comes and trims it. And every now and then they mow the
lawn with a power mower. Makes me feel I'm right in the
thick of things!'

'You idiot,' said Sue, laughing but sympathetic. 'I know
it must be ghastly, but it's only for a little while. You're
so much better.'

'I know,' Bill acknowledged. 'It could be a lot worse. I
count my blessings. There isn't much else to do. Now for
Pete's sake, let's forget my lungs. Tell me about you – and
the kids – and the hospital. That's a snappy outfit you've
got on, my girl.'

'I look all right in my new uniform, too,' Sue told him.

'I've seen you in uniform. I fell in love with you in uniform – in case you've forgotten – but it's a long time since
I've seen you in that inverted teacup you call a cap.'

'Well, it looks just the same. Tabitha adores it.'

'What about the kids? Do they mind your being gone?'

'They did at first, but I'm there all the morning. And anyway, now that school's begun they're so full of it they haven't time to think of anything else.'

'What about my other redhead?'

'Oh, Bill – she's darling! So fat and good.' Sue embarked on a luxurious account of the children, and then moved on to the broader field of Springdale gossip as gleaned from Veazie Ann, who had been to the last town meeting.

'The only first-hand news I've got,' she finished, 'is that the Stuarts are on their way back from Paris. I had a letter from Cal, gibbering because she's missing the first weeks of High School.'

Bill grinned. 'You did a peach of a job on that kid, Sue. Remember what a sulky, stand-offish little beast she was? And now look at her!'

'Well, you helped – and so did she. It'll be nice to have them back. I've missed having near neighbours. I like people around.'

Bill hooted. 'That's pitiful. You're all alone at home, of course, except for four kids and Veazie Ann, but I hadn't realized you were all alone in the hospital. Has everybody walked out?'

'Naturally,' Sue informed him coldly. 'You wouldn't expect the place to run without you, would you?'

'Well, I thought they'd try, at least. Doesn't anybody miss me?'

'Hm. Now let's see – Oh, yes! There's a student on the floor who mourns over you. It seems she worked with you in the Operating Room, and regards you as a kind of surgical Einstein.'

'Well, don't stop. Who is this brilliant child?'

'A senior named Margot Harrison.'

'Harrison? Harris – Oh, sure. I remember her, though

not for the usual reasons. She didn't make mistakes, didn't get rattled, and was always right on the job.'

'Sounds as if the less sensational virtues pay off after all. Anyway, I hope hers do. She's a darned good nurse. Incidentally, she gives every indication of being madly in love with Frank Warren.' She paused, surprised by Bill's scowl.

'Frank,' he said slowly, 'is bad medicine for a serious-minded kid like that.'

'That's what Pat Glennon said, too.'

'What makes you think the kid's in love with him?'

Sue told him about the operating permit and the kiss. Bill groaned.

'Warren and his gestures! Last summer, when Ann Concklin was head nurse in the O.R., he brought her some flowers, bowed from the waist, and said, 'Lace for Queen Ann.' Doesn't sound like much, but it stood Concklin on her ear for two weeks. She didn't know whether she was coming or going.'

'But what's wrong with that?'

'Nothing – except that while the guy likes girls he isn't really thinking about them at all, and he makes gestures like that automatically, with nothing behind them. Unfortunately, it mows the girls down, and meanwhile he's forgotten the gesture *and* the girl.'

Sue considered, frowning. 'What he needs,' she said at last, 'is a good steady wife to keep him out of trouble.'

'Oh-oh!' Bill said. 'I don't like that Mrs Fixit look in your eye. I've seen it before.'

'Nonsense! I wouldn't dream of interfering.'

'Of course you wouldn't, dear. Such a thing never entered your pretty little head. It'll all come about naturally. Well, have fun. If you can fix it so that Frank Warren can tell one pretty girl from another, you're a genius.'

A dimple appeared suddenly at the corner of Sue's mouth; but she said nothing, and after a moment they went on to talk about the hospital in general, about the children, about Springdale, until it was time for Sue to go, and she was faced with the realization that she would not see Bill for another month.

His eyes darkened as she rose, and she was aware of a sudden ache in her throat. There was a brief painful silence before Sue managed a creditable grin.

'Is it safe to leave you here for a month?' she asked lightly. 'I saw a *very* good-looking nurse in the hall as I came in.'

'Don't worry,' Bill returned on the same note. 'One good-looking nurse in my life is all I can manage right now. Later, perhaps –'

'Later I'll deal with it. Meanwhile I'll be slaving on that hot floor while you lie here in your nice cool bed.'

'You love it, and you know it. Aren't you glad, now, that I made you go?'

Sue paused in the doorway and her grin this time was genuine.

'Yes, darling,' she said.

8

When a good nurse makes
a mistake

IF Sue had any serious matchmaking intentions they seemed
likely to die a natural death, for Margot Harrison did not
work the relief shift again for some time. Instead, on
Peggy's evenings off, it was the other student, Marian
Macgraw, who usually came on from seven to eleven, and
she was far less capable than Margot. It was not, Sue
realized, that the girl didn't work steadily, but that, as Pat
said, she didn't take hold.

'I don't get it,' Pat said. 'Marian used to be really good
on the job. Now she just does whatever we tell her to do,
and leaves it at that.'

Sue, when she had time to think about the child, wondered what had brought about the change, but a busy floor,
a busy life at home with the four children, and a constant
inescapable worry about Bill left neither time nor room for
matters which were none of her business.

Meanwhile, she was settling into staff work as if she had
never left it, and her daily drive down the mountain and
across Springdale Valley was now a routine which took
her through a thunder of autumn colours and the smoky
fragrance of burning leaves. At night, coming home to
her sleeping household, the eyes of possum and raccoon
were points of fire from roadside or stone wall, her hands
grew stiff on the cold wheel, and she had her first glimpse

of the great belt of Orion beginning its winter swing across the blue-black sky.

At the hospital, though she was still not certain that she had been wholly accepted by the nurses – with the possible exception of Pat Glennon – she had, for the most part, ceased to worry about it, and went about her work with the comfortable assurance that at least she knew her job.

The evenings, she discovered, had each its own particular overtone, regardless of routine matters.

There were dull evenings when, despite the number of patients or their ailments, nothing happened. Seriously ill patients and convalescent patients, alike, were quiet and uncomplaining. Staff doctors came in and went away again without leaving pages of complicated orders. Interns appeared promptly when called. Even the visitors had no complaints. The telephones were often silent. There were no crises, no alarms, no problems.

There were evenings which could only be described as silly. Patients played practical jokes on each other and on the nurses; visitors brought in plastic candy or rubber fruit; irritable patients were amiable; depressed patients were suddenly cheerful. The usually businesslike Admitting Office developed a tendency to wisecrack on the telephone and announced the arrival of new patients with the statement, 'Hold your hat, dear. We're going to throw the book at you.' Interns jumped at nurses from behind doors. Staff men were hilarious.

There were exasperating evenings, in which patients mislaid false teeth, tried to shave without blades in their razors, upset pitchers of fruit juice in their beds, became entangled in their bathrobes, and involved their wheelchairs with the general furniture. Visitors went into the wrong rooms and were upset. Vases of flowers blew over, cascading water into bureau drawers; refrigerators went wrong and sterilizers overflowed.

There were crazy evenings, in which wives or mothers fainted in the corridors, patients fell out of bed, nurses broke valuable syringes; patients not allowed out of bed were found on the sun porch, while patients who should be up refused to budge. Heart patients had attacks, mild patients quarrelled with their wives and ran up temperatures, emergency cases were admitted with staggering rapidity. Doctors prescribed unknown medicines not in the hospital pharmacy. Interns swarmed, nurses flew, patients, visitors, and nurses developed indignations and bitternesses. Everything was a crisis.

Oddly enough, the pattern, whatever it chanced to be, seemed the same all over the hospital.

'You can count on it,' Pat told Sue. 'A crazy night here is a crazy night all over the house. It's enough to make you believe in voodoo.'

'Maybe it's sunspots, or mass mind,' Sue agreed. 'Or astrology.'

'Or Egyptian prophecies.'

'Could be,' said Sue. 'On the other hand, I can't seem to feel that the Egyptians, or sun-spots, or even Saturn in Snooks could possibly have worked up a thing to make Uncle Billy fall out of bed and then crawl under his bureau and go to sleep.'

'Well, that's so. Or that woman upstairs, the same night, who walked out of her window in her nightgown and went visiting in the neighbourhood.'

Sue was remembering this conversation an afternoon or two later as she came on duty, and she was smiling as she passed Kit's office.

Kit glanced up from her desk at the sound of the light, familiar step.

'What's so funny?' she called.

Sue paused at the door. 'Just nonsense,' she said.

'Well, come in. Don't just stand there. I've got something I want to talk to you about.'

Sue went in and sat down in the chair by the desk.

'What's on your mind?'

'The Macgraw child. Honestly, Sue, I'm worried about that kid. You're always good at getting inside people. What's the matter with her?' Kit's brown eyes were seriously troubled.

'I haven't the faintest idea. What's the story?'

'Well, last year she was one of the best students we had – top marks – adored by patients – cheerful – lots of initiative, and a welcome sight to any head nurse. She's still swell with the patients, but she's lost all the rest. She's being reported to me practically ever hour on the hour – for being inept, indifferent, and inattentive – and she's got some fool notion about not wanting to give medicines. Something *has* to be done about her.'

'Can't you get anywhere talking to her?'

'Not an inch. I can't get through to her. She just sits and quivers and says she'll try to do better – and then doesn't. See if you can find out what it is, will you, Sue?'

'I'll do my best,' Sue promised. 'But I don't guarantee anything. She's very withdrawn, you know.'

'Well, try to un-withdraw her. I'm stumped.'

'Is she on relief today?'

'Yes, from seven o'clock. That's why I brought this up.'

'It may take a while,' Sue warned. 'After all, I'm no miracle worker. I can't just walk up to her, take her by the neck, and squeeze the information out of her.'

'No, I suppose you can't,' Kit admitted. 'Anyway, thanks.'

Sue continued on her way and found Denham unusually quiet. Eight patients had gone home and for once there had been no admissions. 'Looks like an easy night,' she remarked to Pat.

'You never can tell,' Pat returned darkly. 'Keep your fingers crossed. Because we could do with an easy night, for a change. Oh, mercy! Just listen to that, the poor soul.'

'That' was the voice of Mr Rollins, a serious heart case, his condition further complicated by bronchial pneumonia, a raging temperature, and a state of mental excitement which was more than an ordinary delirium. Nothing would quiet him, though everything had been tried. He had not slept for forty-eight hours, nor had he stopped talking for one minute, day or night.

'He drove up here alone, from Florida, the day before he came in,' Miss Patton had explained to Sue and Pat the day before, when she was giving the report. 'And he's still driving. He goes through all the motions with the wheel, with his arms trembling from exhaustion from holding them out in front of him. He just never stops moving, which naturally delays the effect of the penicillin. And you know, his heart is going to give out if we can't get him quiet. Dr Marshall is having a fit. We've got sideboards up, of course, to keep him from falling out of bed.'

'Does he try to get up?' Pat asked.

'No. He's too busy driving that ghastly car. Honestly, after you've listened to him for a while you get so you almost believe in it yourself.'

'Has he got specials?'

'No. His son came in and refused to have them – goodness knows why. Dr Marshall says they have plenty of money. But families are queer. He's in a private room, though. He'd have to be. The other patients couldn't stand it.'

So today, when Sue was making her rounds, she paused a little longer in Mr Rollins's room. He was a distinguished-looking man in his early fifties, his hair just beginning to turn grey; but he was thin and taut, and his eyes, which must normally have been both shrewd and pleasant, stared blindly before him. He said, 'How do you do,' politely, and continued to drive his car, his voice droning on and on – about the road, the scenery, the car.

'Can't you rest for a little while, Mr Rollins?' Sue asked gently.

'No, I'm sorry. I've got to make it to Brunswick before dark if I possibly can.'

'You're in a hospital, Mr Rollins – and in bed.'

'Oh, yes. I know. There've been nurses in and out of here all day. I don't think much of this road, do you? Too much red clay. I've been wondering about that left rear tyre. Do you notice that the car rides a little bumpily on that side?'

Heavens! Sue thought helplessly. She stood there for a moment watching his trembling hands in constant motion with the movement of an imaginary wheel, his right foot shifting from a non-existent brake. Then she turned and went out, her face sober.

A light came on over someone's door and Sue hurried to answer it. You could do something for an acute appendix. Mr Rollins's droning voice followed her along the corridor, faded out in rooms, met her again when she emerged. From time to time, she went back to give him a drink of water or fruit juice and to check his pulse, which was becoming weaker as well as increasingly irregular. He thanked her politely each time, but continued with his driving, and the rise and fall of his voice continued to pursue her.

At seven o'clock Marian Macgraw came on duty and paused at the office, where Sue was charting fluid intakes and outputs.

'Good evening, Mrs Barry. Is Mrs Glennon around?'

Sue nodded. 'She's in the Nurses' Room, having a cup of coffee.'

'Oh.' The girl's tone was dull and so were her eyes. Her face, Sue noticed, looked oddly flat, its planes erased by a complete absence of colour.

Sue tried an experiment. 'Would you like to give the eight o'clock medicines?'

'Oh – *please* – no – I – I mean – of course, Mrs Barry, if you want me to – only I'm terribly slow – and – the meds are pretty – tough – just now, aren't they?'

'Oh, never mind,' said Sue casually, though she was startled by the panic in the girl's voice. 'I'll do the meds. But I wish you'd take a look at Mr Ellery's transfusion. He must be about ready for another bottle.'

Marian Macgraw gasped. '*Transfusion!*' she said, her voice scarcely above a whisper. 'Oh – y-yes.' She clapped a hand over her right eye. 'E-excuse me, Mrs Barry – I – I guess I've got something in my eye.'

She fled, leaving an astonished and very puzzled Sue behind her. What was all this? The child was behaving like a very new and very frightened probationer – and she was in her junior year. It didn't make sense. Well, there was nothing Sue could do about it now. But I'm going to, she promised herself.

It was perhaps an hour later that Sue, carrying a tray of two-ounce glasses in which she had been giving out mineral oil in the ward, took them to the nearest Utility Room to be cleaned, and was vaguely surprised to find the door closed. She pushed it open.

'For heaven's sake!' she exclaimed. 'What's the matter?'

Marian Macgraw was standing in the middle of the Utility Room enveloped in a cloud of steam from the sterilizer. She had a bottle of rubbing alcohol in one hand and a towel in the other. She was crying into the towel.

Sue let the door swing to, behind her; set the tray of glasses on the sink shelf, and put a comforting arm around the girl's shoulders. 'Can't you tell me about it?' she asked.

A pair of red-rimmed eyes looked at her miserably over the towel.

Sue waited while the steam thickened around them. At last she said, 'Come on, my dear. Even if I can't help, it's always better to have someone to talk to. And maybe I *can* help. You never know.'

The student hesitated, swallowed, and then said with difficulty, 'I – I'm trying to get up courage – to ... call my mother ... and tell her I'm going to l-leave training.'

'Leave training!' said Sue, genuinely horrified. 'But why? Don't you like nursing?'

'I – I adore it! I've never wanted to do anything else – *ever*.'

'Then what *is* the trouble?'

The girl drew a long, quivering breath, wiped her eyes with the towel, and said desperately, 'I'm not ... a – a – safe person to ... do this kind of work. I – I ought to get out of it before I kill somebody.'

'Don't talk nonsense,' said Sue sharply. 'You're hysterical!'

'N-no, I'm not, Mrs Barry. Honestly.'

'All right,' said Sue patiently. 'You're not. All the same,

you come over here to the sink, wash your face in some really cold water, blow your nose, and then tell me the whole story.'

The girl shook her head. 'Oh, I – I couldn't, Mrs Barry. I couldn't tell anybody! I'd rather die!'

'Well, you can still splash some cold water on your face.'

'Yes, Mrs Barry.'

She washed her face obediently, dabbed at it with the towel, and looked longingly at the door.

'No,' Sue told her firmly. 'You're going to stay right here and get this off your chest.'

The girl glanced at her almost hopefully. 'You – you won't tell anyone?'

'If it isn't anything that's going to harm either a patient or the hospital – I won't tell anybody.'

Marian's eyes filled again. 'It's only me – now,' she said. 'I – I made a terrible mistake, Mrs Barry. I could have killed someone. It was j-just luck that I didn't.'

'Let's thank luck, then,' said Sue quietly. 'What was it?'

It was a brief but terrifying story, and a chill ran down Sue's back as she listened. Marian Macgraw had been sent to change a transfusion bottle, had taken the fresh bottle from the Utility Room, set it up, and gone on about her work. It was not until the bottle had run out and she was filling out the card on it, in regard to the patient's reaction, if any, that she discovered what she had done.

'It – was the *wrong blood*!' she said with a gasp. 'Only, it wasn't. I mean, it was intended for another patient, but it was the same blood type. Oh, Mrs Barry, if it hadn't been – the patient would have died.'

This was most dreadfully true, for a wrong blood type can cause almost instant death. The girl, however, had suffered too much over her mistake to be lectured now.

'What did you do?' Sue asked.

'I – I did something dishonest. I – changed the labels. The – bottle I should have taken had been sort of pushed behind a flask of saline. That's why I didn't see it the first time. Oh, Mrs Barry, I've hardly slept since. I know I should have reported it – but I was so horrified – and no harm had been done. They were both type O. Only, I haven't been able to think of anything else since; and I've got so I'm scared to give medicines, or even take around trays at mealtime, because I might give a diabetic or somebody the wrong tray.'

'No,' said Sue. 'You won't. I don't think you'll ever make a mistake again. Truly. When a good nurse makes a mistake like that, it's burned into her. You were a good nurse before this happened. You should be a better one now. Believe me, my dear, you are undoubtedly the safest nurse we have, when it comes to giving medicines.'

Hope flared in the child's eyes and died down again – almost. A spark was left, but she had been under a self-induced strain for so long that she was unable to adjust to this new point of view.

'I hope so, Mrs Barry,' she said. She shuddered. 'If only I could make up for it some way maybe I'd feel okay again – but how can I? I did a terribly wrong thing – and he could have died. I can't get away from that, And *I can't make up for it* – ever! I – I still think I'd better leave training.'

'Wait a little and see how you feel,' Sue counselled.

'I won't feel any differently,' the student said grimly. 'But thank you for being so kind, Mrs Barry. It *has* helped, to talk to someone.' She turned slowly, pushed open the door, and went out.

Sue's face and hair were beaded with moisture from the

fog of steam. She caught the door back, flung up a window, and with a swab of alcohol began methodically to clean the oily glasses. It was too bad, she thought, that the kid's mistake hadn't come out at the time. A swift penalty imposed by the Nursing School Office would have been much healthier for her than this prolonged, morbid self-punishment.

When Sue had finished the glasses she returned them to the medicine cabinet just as the stumpy figure of Mr Rollins's physician, Dr Marshall, came down the corridor and turned in at the office. Pat handed him the chart and Sue came to the door, anxious to know what his opinion might be.

The doctor sat down, went over the chart carefully, and rubbed his forehead. Then he turned to Pat.

'Has he slept at all?'

'No, sir. The morphine didn't touch him and neither did the paraldehyde. He's still driving.'

'Oh-oh!' The doctor rested his elbows on the desk and leaned his head on his hands. Presently he said, as much to himself as to the girls, 'If he doesn't have rest — with that badly decompensated heart . . .' He pushed back his chair and rose. 'Well,' he said, 'let's go and have a look at him.'

Pat gave Sue a glance which said clearly that she was rushed to death, and would Sue go with Dr Marshall?

So they went down the corridor into the increasing sound of Mr Rollins's voice; but they paused, instinctively, outside the door, for another voice — Marian Macgraw's — was saying:

'Why don't you get over on the back seat, Mr Rollins, and get some rest? I'll drive. I'm really a very good driver.'

'Maybe I will after a while. Let's just get through this town first, and then we'll see. It's good of you to come with me. I was getting rather lonely.'

'Well, it was good of you to pick me up. Most people are afraid of hitch-hikers. And I can promise you I won't run off with your car if you'd like to have a nap.'

'Oh, I can see that. You've got a nice, honest face.'

Sue and Dr Marshall stood motionless, staring at one another and waiting.

Mr Rollins's voice went on. It was no longer a drone, but was definitely conversational.

'Wouldn't you like some coffee?' he asked. 'I'm getting hungry, myself. There's a drugstore on that corner – see it? Just beyond the stoplight. Why don't we stop there?'

'I'd love to. I could do with a sandwich.'

'So could I. Ha! That light changed at exactly the right instant!'

There was a pause. Then the girl's voice said gaily, 'I'll have coffee with you on one condition: that you do what I asked when we come out – go over on the back seat and let me drive for a while.'

'All right, it's a bargain! Here we are. Look out – don't catch your fingers in the door. Seems a nice clean place, doesn't it? . . . How do you do, sir? Two coffees, and two chicken sandwiches, please. No, thank you – we'll have them right here at the counter.'

Sue and Dr Marshall waited, fascinated. The illusion of the drugstore, the sandwiches, and the coffee was becoming so real that Sue would not have been surprised if Dr Marshall had stepped forward and ordered two more coffees.

Meanwhile they listened – through the coffee and the sandwiches. The latter, it seemed, were only passable. At last Marian and Mr Rollins slid down off the stools and emerged, only to engage in an argument on the sidewalk – as to whether or not Marian should pay Mr Rollins for her own meal.

'Nonsense!' Mr Rollins said firmly. 'Let's hear no more about it.'

The girl gave in gracefully and Mr Rollins seemed to be opening the car door for her.

'Oh, no!' she said quickly. 'You *promised*. *You* are going to stretch out in the back and *I* am going to drive.'

'Did I? Don't you think – perhaps – a little later . . . ?'

'No, I don't. You've been driving for hours and you're tired to death. I know the road. And even if you don't go to sleep – if you just relax for a while and rest – it'll make all the difference. Please! You said you would.'

There was a long silence, in which Sue held her breath. Then Mr Rollins laughed good-naturedly. 'All right,' he said. 'You win. I never could refuse a nice girl when she says "Please" like that. Here – take the keys. This one is the ignition.'

There was another pause. Then Marian said, 'Are you comfortable back there?'

'Perfectly, thank you.'

'Good! Now I don't want to hear a word out of you.'

He stretched luxuriously and yawned. 'This wasn't a bad idea at all,' he murmured.

'Hush,' said Marian, as one would say to a child.

There was another silence, and this one continued. A full minute passed, and then another. Dr Marshall edged toward the crack in the half-open door and looked in. A broad, relieved grin spread over his face. 'By Godfreys! She's done it!' He motioned to Sue and they crept away. 'He's sleeping like a baby,' he said. 'Who's that student?'

Sue told him just as Marian Macgraw tiptoed out of the room drawing the door softly to behind her, and came down the corridor.

'Miss Macgraw!' Dr Marshall said.

She paused, still preoccupied and looking somewhat dazed. 'Yes, sir?'

'That was a beautiful piece of work you just pulled off. We heard it. How did you happen to think of that dodge?'

'Oh – why, it was simple enough, sir. He was so exhausted that I knew if I could only get him on to the back seat he'd go to sleep.'

'You knew it, did you? How did you know it?'

The girl looked startled. 'Why – er – why – I just *did*.'

'So!' said the doctor. 'Very interesting – and very rare. Had your mental nursing yet?'

'No, sir.'

'Hm. Well, you have an exceptional talent for it. Better consider it. People like you are badly needed in that field. There's a future in it, you know. You'll do well. I shall speak to your Director of Nurses about you at once.'

The dazed look was gone from Marian's face and a warm tide of colour swept over it.

'Th-thank you, sir,' she stammered.

The doctor nodded. 'It's less than you deserve. If *somebody* hadn't done the right thing, he would have died.' Still beaming, he returned to the office, leaving Sue and Marian facing one another in the corridor.

'But,' said Sue, meeting the girl's eyes, 'somebody *did* do the right thing, and he *didn't* die. That sort of squares things, doesn't it?'

'*What?* Why – yes, it does!' She gave Sue one quick glance of happiness and turned away.

'Macgraw!' Sue called after her with sudden inspiration – 'Will you give out the nine o'clock meds, please?'

The girl turned back long enough to answer, 'I'd *love* to, Mrs Barry!' Then she was gone – on feet which barely touched the floor.

9

Nurses

IN mid-November Sue heard that Lot Phinney was ill, and she telephoned to inquire about it.

'It's a lot of consarned nonsense!' he told her. 'I wish Bill was home!'

'But what *is* it?' Sue insisted.

He hesitated. Then, 'Well, Doc Mason claims it's my heart. Don't seem to amount to much. All I done was shift my twenty-foot extension ladder to the front gable, so's I could clean out my gutters. I got kinder short of breath, that was all, so I layed down for a minute. Then that numb-skull of an Ellie Dimmick that's keeping house for me, she up and called Doc Mason without a-telling me.' He paused.

'Well?' said Sue.

' 'Twarn't well. That fool Mason said I was to stay abed.'

'So naturally you got up at once.'

'Sartin I did. I ain't got time to sit around a-holding hands with my blood-pressure.'

'Now you listen to me, Lot Phinney. Did the doctor say you had a coronary?'

'He give it some such name, but all it boils down to is a mite of a blood clot. Stands to reason that's going to clear up. It don't bother me none.'

'That's just great,' said Sue. 'And I suppose you're busy, as usual?'

'I be – and don't you git to worrying, Sue.'

Two days later the ambulance brought him to the hospital. He had been jacking up his car on the highway, to change a flat tyre, and a State Trooper had found him there, lying on the road beside the jack. He was in Room 9 in an oxygen tent when Sue came on duty and she went to see him as soon as the report was finished. He was lying high on his pillows, still breathing with difficulty, and his face was a blue-grey. Sue stood at the foot of the bed and looked at him in helpless distress. He glared back irritably through the transparency of the plastic oxygen tent. Neither spoke for a moment. Then Lot said, 'Well, here I be.'

'I'd noticed, and I'm thankful. Now you'll *have* to take care of yourself.'

There was a flicker of relief in Lot's eyes, too, though he replied from force of habit, 'Well, *I* ain't thankful.'

'Are you in any pain?'

'Some. Nothing to brag about, though 'twas a ring-tailed peeler for a while.' He paused, out of breath, and after a moment Sue left him to rest.

He would, she thought after studying his chart, be out of the tent in about a week, if he didn't have another attack, and the next six weeks in bed ought to impress him, as nothing else had done, with the necessity for taking care of himself.

He did not have another attack, and in due time the tent was removed and he was allowed to feed himself, to everyone's relief. Lot had not responded cheerfully to being fed. Now, however, with a small amount of his independence regained, he became a surprisingly good patient, uncomplaining and interested in everything.

His room-mate, Abel Torrey, was a quiet, gentle old

man from one of the remote farms among the hills. He had broken his leg in a fall from his own haymow. Lot had known him all his life, but never well until now, and he worried far more about the old man than he did about himself.

Mr Torrey rarely asked for anything, but lay quietly all day with heavy weights attached to his leg, and he did not complain about pain, smiling gently at the nurses who gave him his bath or made his bed. Everyone was fond of him – with the exception of one young graduate, a Miss Watson, who was not fond of anybody, and who left a trail of vague discomfort wherever she went.

Miss Watson did her work conscientiously, with great attention to detail, but she was fretful about it and made the patients feel that they were almost unbearable nuisances. When she worked on the relief shift, Sue and Pat spent much of their time soothing irritated men.

It was a week or two after Lot had come out of his oxygen tent, and was beginning to feel a little more like himself, that Miss Watson was on duty from seven in the evening until eleven. She came on with a long face, as usual; grumbled steadily about everything she had to do, and repeated at frequent intervals: 'The patients on this floor are enough to drive anybody crazy.'

The heavier routine of the evening was nearly finished and the nurses were beginning to relax their steady drive when a light came on over Mr Torrey's door. Miss Watson moaned and went to answer it, returning to the office presently with an air of satisfaction.

'Well,' she announced to Sue and Pat, who were starting work on the charts, 'I guess I've settled that! Can you imagine it – at this hour he decides he's hungry and wants tea and toast!'

Pat looked up quickly. 'Who does?' she asked.

'That old Mr Torrey! He didn't eat any supper, *he* says – so now he's hungry! I told him – I said, "We haven't time to cook extra meals for all the patients. If you can't eat your supper when it's set before you, you'll just have to go without." Tea and toast at this hour!'

There was a silence. Then Pat swung around in her chair. 'Look, Watson,' she said. 'Has it ever struck you that it's very poor nursing practice to let any patient see that you're annoyed with him? Mr Torrey never asks for *anything*. He couldn't eat his supper because he was having a lot of pain. I gave him codeine for it, and *I* told him that if he wanted anything later to let us know. But even if I hadn't, there was no reason to bawl the old man out like that!'

Miss Watson's mouth went down at the corners. 'Well, of course, if you feel like that, Mrs Glennon – you're in charge here – so I suppose I'll have to fix him something – though really, if we're going to spend all our time cooking for the patients, I don't see –'

'Never mind!' Sue exploded before Pat could reply. 'If you took him anything now it would probably choke him. I'll get it.' She rose and went to the kitchen. 'Practically the first thing he's asked for,' she muttered under her breath as she started the toaster and put some water on for tea. It was no wonder that people went out of hospitals saying that nurses were unfeeling. 'If she'd even refused politely . . .!' said Sue furiously as she reached for a small tray.

She took the tea and toast to the unhappy Mr Torrey, who accepted it with almost tearful gratitude.

'I'm real sorry,' he told her. 'I didn't mean to make no trouble.'

'You didn't. I was delighted to get it for you.' Sue turned to encounter Lot Phinney's enraged eyes.

'That long-faced ninny orter lose her job!' he snapped. 'Coming in here and talking to a nice old feller that way. If I'd of had my legs under me I'd of give her a smacking where 'twould of done the most good!'

'Take it easy,' Sue warned him. 'If you get excited you'll have a setback.'

'That's right, Lot,' Mr Torrey said anxiously. 'The girl didn't mean no harm. Likely she was tired. These nurses work awful hard, and 'twarn't very considerate of me.'

'Nonsense –' Sue began, and was interrupted by Lot.

'Maybe she didn't mean no harm,' Lot said, 'but she done harm all the same. A nurse ain't got no call to go around punishing folks for not eating their supper. I thought this was a hospital – not a reform school.'

Sue was in hearty agreement with this, and as there was nothing she could say in defence of Miss Watson she retreated to the office, where she found Pat alone.

'I'd like to shake Watson,' Sue told her.

'So would I . . . I've nearly finished the charts, Sue. Do you want to put the narcotics in the report?'

'Sure.' Sue pulled out a chair and settled down to work, but in spite of her concentration on the narcotics she found herself nursing a second line of thought. What was the matter with the nurses like Watson? For there were others – most of them young, Sue realized. Was it a youthful lack of imagination and experience in life which made them unable, even remotely, to put themselves in the patient's place or understand his feelings? The hospital, to them, was so familiar that they couldn't seem to comprehend its being frightening. But *why* couldn't they?

Was I ever like that? Sue wondered, horrified. I

couldn't have been, not with Miss Cameron on my neck.

But surely, it must be apparent to anyone with reason that the patient, his normal life disrupted and his worries increased by his illness, would find the hospital a terrifying alien place, where he would know neither what to expect, nor what was expected of him.

Anybody, Sue reflected, could get along with a nice patient. What these kids didn't grasp was that the difficult patient was the real challenge to their nursing ability. Instead, they fell into the habit of expecting the utmost in amiability from every patient, until in the end they began to think that even a gentle old soul like Mr Torrey was a pest.

'Where did Watson train?' she asked Pat suddenly.

'I don't know. Not a very good school, I should think. In my hospital the patient's feelings came before the nurse's. We had that ground into us with an axe, from the very first day.'

'Me, too,' said Sue with a reminiscent grin, and there was a silence, broken only by the busy scratching of two pens.

A little later, just before Sue went off duty, she glanced into Lot's room. A small nightlight was on between the beds and in the semi-darkness both men appeared to be asleep. Then Lot stirred. 'Sue?'

'Yes.' She tiptoed to the bed to say good night.

'I'm kinder sorry I was so cantankerous,' Lot whispered. 'Not but what I'd've been more so, far's that girl's concerned, but after you left I give Abel what-for, for being so all-fired meek. I — It kind of upset him. I wisht my infernal tongue didn't git away from me.'

Sue nodded, aware that this was the burden which most outspoken people must bear — that they so often bruised when they meant to be kind, and distressed when they meant to strengthen.

'Don't worry, Lot,' she said gently. 'Even if it upset him for a minute I know he understands. I've never minded your barking, and anyway, I'm interested in your point of view on nurses. It's hard for us, you know, to get the patient's angle. I've never had a personal friend, as a patient, who wasn't in the medical profession, so I'm glad to know how things seem to you.'

'Well,' said Lot, 'I guess you're likely to.'

Sue was not, however, to hear any more of Lot's opinions of nurses until Abel Torrey went home, to be tended by his wife and the Visiting Nurse. The day after Abel's departure Lot acquired a new room-mate, a boy of nineteen with a sudden and serious kidney infection. He was a visitor in the White Mountains and his parents, notified by wire of his illness, hurried to Springdale demanding a private room and special nurses. The nurses were available, but there was no unoccupied private room, so Johnnie Becket remained with Lot, who lay quietly watching everything that went on.

The boy's three-o'clock-to-eleven special nurse had been on the floor on another case and Sue remembered her with pleasure, not only because she didn't make work for the staff nurses, but because Sue thought her excellent. Lot would see some extra good nursing now, and it would be fun to know what he thought.

Lot, however, when Sue mentioned Miss Jordan, was oddly non-committal. 'She's a nice girl, and she tries real hard,' was all he would say, leaving Sue surprised and puzzled.

Miss Jordan was small, slim, and wiry, with smooth brown hair under the white flare of her cap, and she had very bright brown eyes, almost like a bird's, Sue thought. She was very quick in her movements and very kind, taking infinite pains with her patient and also with his family, talking to them at length outside the room, explaining and consoling. Johnnie's family was grateful and clung to her.

Then Johnnie lost consciousness and Miss Jordan's face began to look strained, almost haunted.

'It's tragic,' she said once to Sue, in the Nurses' Room. 'I don't think he has a chance, and he's so young, and the only one they have.' Her eyes filled with tears.

It was later that same evening that Lot offered his first real comment. Johnnie's parents were sitting wearily in the solarium, Miss Jordan had gone to supper, and Sue was keeping an eye on the unconscious boy in the meantime.

'That girl,' said Lot suddenly, 'had ought to git a hold on her feelings. She's scaring Johnnie's folks half to death.'

Sue turned, astonished. 'What on earth do you mean?'

'I mean she's a-taking this too hard. It's a real good thing for a nurse to feel for her patient and his folks, but 'tain't a good thing for her to feel like he was her blood kin. Maybe Johnnie's going to pull through, and maybe he ain't, but whichever way it goes, his folks need somebody round to lean on. Way that nurse is, they'll be a-holding *her* up.'

At this moment Miss Jordan rushed back into the room, having taken fifteen minutes for supper, and Sue left, but Lot's unexpected and shrewd comment had startled her, and she began to pay more attention to Miss Jordan's comings and goings. Miss Jordan, she noticed, no longer hurried in and out of the room – she ran, followed by the terrified eyes of Johnnie's parents. The never-forgotten words of Miss Cameron, Sue's Nursing Arts instructor, came back across the years:

'A nurse should always walk. *Never run!* It suggests fear.'

Johnnie Becket didn't die; he recovered. But long before he was moved to a private room, he was beginning to be fretful with Miss Jordan. 'I'm okay,' he kept saying. 'I'm *okay*, Miss Jordan! Why don't you sit down a minute?'

Miss Jordan replied tenderly that being cross was always a sign of convalescence.

' ''Twarn't convalescence,' Lot told Sue after Johnnie had been moved. 'He wasn't like that with his other two nurses. I'd hate to have that girl taking care of me. She's always a-panting.'

'Just the same, she's not as bad as Miss Watson,' Sue pointed out.

'What ye mean — not as bad? She's a sight *worse*! T'other one only makes ye mad, and she'll likely outgrow it. This one scares ye to death — and she ain't a-going to outgrow it.'

'Oh, dear,' said Sue, laughing. 'Aren't any of us any good?'

'Dunno,' said Lot, his eyes twinkling. 'Remains to be seen.'

IO

The remainder

THERE was heavy snow on Mt Washington, now, and on most of the upper slopes of the hills; but Springdale, in its warm valley, with its river, could still boast bare ground.

'It's pneumonia time – 'flu time – tonsillitis time,' Sue told Bill on her monthly visit to him. 'Just pray that the children don't get any of them.'

'I'll do my best,' Bill promised. 'How's my baby red-head?'

'Fat and sassy! Oh, Bill, she's going to be crawling before long! Even now, when you put her on the floor, she humps up her little rear-end and rocks back and forth on her hands and knees. She doesn't know, yet, what she's trying for, but it makes her awfully mad because she can't do it.'

Bill's hearty laugh rang out and Sue studied his face. He had certainly put on weight, and his skin was clear. He looked better than he had in several years, she thought, her heart lifting, but she didn't dare ask when he would be coming home. He probably didn't know, anyway, and there was no use even asking, really, before the first of March. That seemed very far away, and Christmas would not be Christmas without him. She turned her mind resolutely away from this thought, but it cropped up again in spite of her, as she was driving home.

Stop it! she told herself sharply. He's getting well, and

he's in better spirits than he's been since he went over there. I ought to be thankful instead of complaining.

She was, nevertheless, very glad to find an unusually busy floor waiting for her when she returned to the hospital. On her way in she encountered Pat, looking very rosy and much younger than her years.

'Hi,' Pat said cheerfully, and they went on together, glancing somewhat apprehensively at the Emergency Room, which was a scene of violent activity.

'Oh-oh!' said Sue. 'I'll bet we're going to have a tough night.'

'Looks like it,' Pat agreed.

Denham Two, when they reached it, had a littered appearance entirely foreign to it, and the day nurses looked up with glazed eyes at Sue as Pat went past the office to the Nurses' Room.

When they came out for the report, Miss Patton greeted them wearily. 'Seven post-operatives,' she said, 'and all of them ought to have somebody with them. One hasn't come down yet – just went up, in fact. He's a tonsillectomy – man about thirty – and he'll have to go in with Mr Phinney, it's the last bed we have. Oh, and you'll be happy to know that, aside from remaining constantly at the bedside of all seven post-operatives, you have an irrigation which must be done every ten minutes for twenty-four hours. It takes at least fifteen minutes to do it.'

'Oh, that's all right,' Pat said airily, 'if Sue and Peggy and Eben and I can become seven people, we may as well become eight.'

'I haven't finished,' said Miss Patton. 'You have three blood-pressures to be taken every hour until stable, two patients who think they're somewhere else and keep trying to get out of bed to go to the hospital – you have to stay with them, too – and there's a three-hundred-pound man in a plaster cast from his neck to his hip – fractured spine. He has to be turned every two hours. Aside from that, you have nothing to do except your regular work.'

'Wow!' Pat said. 'Let's go home, Sue!'

'Just wait till I get my coat,' Sue told her.

Miss Patton regarded them sourly. Her usually smooth hair was in wisps, her uniform was rumpled and stained. and there was a splash of gentian violet on one of her white shoes. It was a large splash and unlikely to come off.

'You're revolting, both of you,' she said, and turned to the day staff. 'Look at them, girls! Coming in here all starched and immaculate, with not a hair out of place! I hate you.'

Pat grinned, and Sue remarked comfortably, 'Cheer up! We won't look like this when we go off duty.'

'You're darned right, you won't,' the day shift said happily. 'Well, so long, girls. Have a nice, nice evening! *We're* going home!'

They trooped off the floor, white with exhaustion but laughing happily.

Sue and Pat and Peggy looked at one another. Eben had already vanished in answer to a light.

'Well, kids,' Pat said, 'on your mark!'

It was, as expected, a tough evening, but not one which they would particularly remember, since there had been others like it, and would be more. Sue, in fact, would not have remembered it for two days if it hadn't been for the tonsillectomy.

His name was Harold St John, and a burlier young man Sue never hoped to see – nor a more co-operative one, all things considered.

His return from the operating room was uneventful. He

arrived, still unconscious, was put to bed, his doctor issued the usual routine orders, his wife came to sit with him – to the girls' relief – and Lot remarked that he knew Harry, who was a truck driver for a grain and feed company in Winslow.

Harry recovered from the anaesthetic in an hour or two – with a very sore throat, but otherwise in good shape. Sue brought him a bowl of cracked ice; and, in view of the general situation on the floor, showed young Mrs St John where she could find more cracked ice, and how to fill the ice collar.

'We're a little rushed,' Sue explained.

'Oh, that's all right,' the girl assured her. 'I'm real glad to have something to do for him.'

Poor Harry looked miserably from one to the other, tried to speak and failed, tried to swallow and cringed.

'I'll keep watch of him, Sue,' Lot said. 'Get along about your work.'

Sue grinned at him and plunged back into the floor work with Pat, Peggy and Eben taking patients out of ether beds, changing draw sheets, racing to do the irrigation, wiping sweaty faces, answering lights, giving hypodermics, hurrying to do the irrigation, serving trays, changing coffee-pots for teapots, and tea for coffee, getting more bread slices, hurrying to do the irrigation while Pat hurried to take the blood-pressures, and everybody tried to watch all the post-operatives and keep the two wandering patients in bed. It required the united efforts of all four to turn the three-hundred-pound man in his cast, but he was turned, faithfully, every two hours – or nearly.

The backrubs that night were sketchy, but the patients, hearing, as patients always do, that the 'girls' were rushed, made no complaint and asked for very little.

They're sweet, Sue thought, dashing to the medicine cabinet for some antacid powder. I suppose I'm tired, but there's one thing about it – I haven't had time to notice.

'Mrs Barry?' said a voice behind her.

Sue turned, to see the very white face and terrified eyes of young Mrs St John.

'What is it?' Sue asked gently.

'Mr Phinney said I should get you. Seems like Harry's kind of bleeding.'

Oops! Sue thought, but aloud she said casually, 'Well, don't worry. Tonsillectomies do that, you know. But I'll check and see. You go on back, and I'll be right with you.' Sue snatched a flashlight from the closet, and as soon as Mrs St John had disappeared into Room 9 hurried in search of anybody. She found Peggy.

'Stick around, Peggy – I think Mr St John is having a haemorrhage.'

'Okay,' said Peggy as Sue dashed into the Treatment Room for a pair of long-handled forceps and a can of sterile sponges – not that she'd need them, she hoped, but you could never be sure.

'Just wait by the door, Peggy,' said Sue. 'If I nod you can go on about your business, but if I just look at you – go and get Mrs Glennon *at once!*'

Sue went into Room 9, her face unconcerned, tossed a cheerful comment at Lot, and came to stand beside Harold St John's bed. One glance at the basin full of bright blood was enough. Sue turned and her eyes met Peggy's in urgent command.

Peggy vanished.

Sue smiled at Mrs St John, said comfortably to the patient, 'Let's have a look at this – if you don't mind sitting up.'

He sat up, opened his mouth obediently, though with

an effort, and Sue turned the flashlight on the hot, swollen tunnel of his throat. She was aware that Pat was behind her now and seeing with her the rhythmic, pumping spurt from a tiny artery on the left side of the throat.

'Taste salt?' she asked and the man nodded.

'I'm afraid,' Sue told him, 'that I'm going to have to hurt you for a minute, Mr St John. I'm sorry.'

He made an unintelligible sound of acquiescence and Sue, as gently as she could, placed the gauze sponge against the pumping artery – and pressed hard. There was agony in the man's eyes but he neither flinched nor made a sound.

'Good work,' Sue told him, and smiled at his wife, who smiled back, not understanding at all, but no longer frightened.

Just when Pat left, Sue didn't know – only that she had gone – to call an intern, Sue knew.

After a full minute she removed the sponge and looked in. The throat was dry and clean. She rolled up the head of the bed, and Mr St John leaned back against it.

'Don't talk,' Sue warned him. 'Here!' She ladled a spoon-ful of cracked ice into his mouth. 'Better keep that going,' she advised. Then, to his wife, 'He's really all right, but we're going to give him something to stop the pain and make him sleep, so why don't you go home and get some sleep yourself?'

'I guess I will,' the girl said gratefully. 'Seems like he tries to talk when I'm here, and maybe that was what –'

Sue laughed. 'Of course, he wants to talk to you. But honestly, he ought to go to sleep.'

Thank you so much, Mrs Barry. You've been real kind. Good night, Harry – see you tomorrow.'

By the time the intern arrived on the floor, Mrs St John had left, Pat had given the uncomfortable Harry a codeine hypodermic and, as far as Room 9 was concerned, all was peace.

'You sure he was bleeding?' the intern demanded.

'Come look at the basin,' Pat said.

'Oh – well – never mind.'

Sue watched the throat carefully for the next hour but there was no more bleeding, and the last time Sue went in, Harold St John was asleep.

'Well,' Lot said, as Sue was tiptoeing out, 'I guess that's the remainder.'

'Remainder?' said Sue, her mind on the overdue irrigation.

'I told ye, when ye said wasn't any of ye any good, that it remained to be seen. Ye done good, Sue, you and Mrs Glennon. Cool as cucumbers, both of ye, and real kind. Made that boy and his wife feel like he was in good hands and everything was dandy. That's how it orter be. But ye didn't fool me none. I seen that blood. Come near to being a bad one, didn't it?'

'If you know so much,' Sue retorted, 'why ask me?'

She ducked out the door before he could reply.

Some time later Pat dropped the last chart into the rack and put down her pen.

'I'd like to tell you something, Sue,' she began.

'What?'

'You're a damned good nurse.'

There are, for a nurse, no sweeter words in the English language, and Sue flushed with pleasure and gratitude. 'Thank you, Pat,' she replied simply. 'So are you.'

'I hope I am. But look – there's something else. I don't suppose you knew it, but when you first came the whole staff was sort of jittery about you, if you follow me.'

'Yes. I – I'm afraid I do.' Sue hesitated, and then said slowly, 'Are you still?'

'No. That's what I wanted to tell you. It took us about two weeks to realize that you were absolutely all right – no wife-of-the-Chief-of-Staff business, and no stuff about being Miss Van Dyke's best friend. You came in here, and went to work, and kept your mouth shut. It's actually hard, now, for us to remember how we felt. Everybody thinks you're swell, Sue. I – I thought you'd like to know.'

II

Everybody's troubles

'DENHAM TWO, Mrs Barry speaking,' said Sue automatically
into the telephone. Then, 'Oh, hello, Frank. What's on your
mind?'

'Hello, Mrs B,' said Frank Warren's voice. 'Is Margot
up to her neck, or can I talk to her for a minute?'

'She's right here.' Sue handed Margot the telephone.

For a moment Margot looked happy, but as she listened
the brightness drained from her face. Her voice, however,
remained casual.

'Of course, it's all right,' she said. 'I think it's swell
Mackin asked for you. Oh, don't be silly! You know per-
fectly well I understand. Remember me? I work here, too.
Well, see you around.'

She hung up carefully and turned away, her lipstick a
bright stain on an otherwise colourless face.

'Wait a minute, Margot,' said Sue. 'Anything wrong?'

'Nothing,' Margot replied grimly, 'except to me. Dr
Warren and his career! This is the second time he's stood
me up in a month!'

'Well,' Sue pointed out, 'it's something that he makes
the dates in the first place. Seems to me you've at last
reached first base.'

'I want to be a lot farther than first base,' Margot
said, half to herself, and then added hastily, 'but naturally,
if Dr Mackin really wants him for that gastroenterostomy

tomorrow afternoon, Frank can't very well take me out for the afternoon and dinner. But it leaves me with a lot of time off to kill. I suppose I can always catch up on my mending, or go for a nice bracing walk.'

'Don't,' Sue advised her. 'I'm off tomorrow, too. Come on home with me, tonight. We're having a mild sort of celebration tomorrow afternoon. My next-door neighbours have just come back from Paris — Mona Stuart and her daughter, Cal. Maybe you've heard of Mrs Stuart. She's an artist.'

'Oh, I *have*,' said Margot, brightening. 'She was having an exhibition at the Modern Art Museum in New York the first and only time I was ever there.'

'Well, don't let her frighten you. She's really a wonderful person, but she can be ruder than anyone I ever met in my life. Not that she means to be. I guess she can't help it. Just keep telling yourself that she has a heart of gold under that rude exterior.'

'I'll do that,' Margot promised. 'Oh, I'd love to come home with you, Mrs Barry — but I'll have to call our house mother, first.'

As it happened, there was no need for Sue's warning about Mona Stuart, who behaved with a courtesy which would have been entirely unnatural to her when she first came to Springdale, less than two years ago. Then, she had been a curt, disagreeable woman, snapping at her employees, and announcing loudly that she asked nothing of the world except to be let alone. It was an attitude which had left her beautiful fourteen-year-old daughter, Cal, with a seriously twisted outlook. The child had felt unwanted, alone, and savagely bitter about her beauty, which, she was convinced, was the only thing about her that interested either her mother or anyone else.

In despair, she had turned to Sue, who had worked hard,

and at last effectually, to straighten out the situation. It was through Sue's efforts that Cal gradually learned to associate with other young people, to go to dances and the movies, and had acquired a normal amount of poise for her age. The winter before, she had been one of the most popular girls at Springdale High School; and she had enjoyed every minute of it.

Mrs Stuart, oddly enough, had expanded, too, and this afternoon she listened, fascinated while Veazie Ann brought her up to date on the local news.

'. . . Seventy-eight years old if he's a day,' Sue heard, 'and dead drunk. He clumb off the bus and laid right down in the road behind it. Couldn't nobody budge him till the minister happened by in his car. He's a young feller and awful strong. They say he picked Silas up like he was a sack of beans and lugged him into the Ventresses' kitchen. There warn't nothing the Ventresses could do but keep him, seeing as 'twas the minister brought him. They say Silas raised Cain all night, a-whooping and a-hollering on the kitchen floor. . . . Tom and Lura never got a wink of sleep. And then, come morning, Silas he got up off the floor, and he hollers, "Where's my coffee? I never see a woman yet could do anything on time." Lura was so mad it's a wonder she didn't pizen him. She's still a-jawing about it.'

As Mona Stuart's booming laugh rang out Sue glanced across the room at Cal, who, with Margot, was lounging comfortably on the couch. Margot's dark hair and blue eyes, though charming, could not make her the beauty which Cal undeniably was. There was, however, more in the young nurse's face than mere prettiness – it had intelligence and integrity, and she was not overshadowed even by Cal's shining golden hair and slanting grey eyes.

Cal, Sue noted with satisfaction, had outgrown her blue-jeans phase. The clothes which she had obviously acquired in Paris — rose-coloured blouse and well-cut black slacks — became her perfectly.

It was evident that, despite the difference in ages, the two girls were congenial. Cal's cosmopolitan life had given her a maturity, which Margot could respect. Cal, on her part, was open in her admiration of Margot's status as a fully-fledged senior nurse, and listened, awed, to Margot's hospital stories. Both were outspoken in their admiration of Sue.

'She's wonderful,' Cal said. 'Honestly, I think she saved my *life*! I was so mixed up I didn't know which from what — and then she came along and everything that hadn't made sense . . . did.'

'She's like that,' Margot agreed. 'You should see her at the hospital. The patients are crazy about her; and after she's coped with some of our old fusspots for a while, they suddenly get human with all of us. I don't know how she does it.'

Sue, who was listening with one ear, was amused. She took the conversation for what it was worth — the idealistic outpouring of the very young. It was when her children — except the baby, who was asleep — made an entrance that Sue lost her detachment and became, as Kit or Bill would have pointed out, the shamelessly proud mother.

Johnny, who for a year now had been steadfastly insisting that he was going to be a doctor, had operated on his toy horse and had deftly clipped the stomach together with Bill's stapler. He solemnly displayed his patient and everyone agreed that he had done a masterly job of surgery.

Then Jerry offered to play the piano. His highly unusual musical talent had never been forced because Sue and Bill wanted him to have a normal childhood, but he was always happiest at the piano, and now he played his newest offering, a little Chopin waltz, with what his teacher had assured Sue was a maturity far beyond his years.

Tabitha, too, Sue reflected, was a credit to her, though the child's gifts of sound common sense and natural poise were less apparent at the moment than her delicate prettiness. She looked particularly charming in her red corduroy dress with its white Eton collar; her shining black pigtails, tied with red ribbons, bobbed endearingly.

'Come here, darling,' said Sue. 'One of your hair ribbons is loose.'

'I'm all right, Mummy, thank you,' Tabitha said and leaned against Cal's knee. 'Cal, can't you come and see my rabbits? We've got six new baby ones.'

Cal gave her an absent-minded hug with one arm. 'Not just now, honey,' she said. 'I'm talking to Margot.'

'But they're so *cunning*!'

'I'll see them tomorrow, Tabs.' She turned back to Margot.

Tabitha moved disconsolately away and Sue ached for her. When Cal had first come to Springdale she had been Tabitha's constant companion, since she distrusted her own contemporaries. Now Cal had grown up. She was fifteen and a young lady leaving Tabitha desolate in childhood.

'Tabs, dear,' said Sue, 'would you like to pass the sandwiches?'

'No, thank you, Mummy.'

'But why, darling? You've always loved to do things like that.'

'Anybody can pass sandwiches,' Tabitha said, flatly.

'Tabs, come here!' said the astounded Sue, and drawing

the child against her, whispered a few reminders about hospitality and making guests feel at home.

'All right, Mummy,' Tabitha said and for the remainder of the afternoon she remembered her manners and seemed contented. It was not until Sue was helping Margot collect her belongings before driving her to the hospital that shrieks of rage suddenly re-echoed from the living-room, accompanied by thuds.

'It's the boys,' Sue explained wearily. 'They start out wrestling for fun, and then one of them hurts the other and you have the real thing. I'll have to separate them.'

But it was not the twins who were fighting – it was Tabitha and Jerry, rolling frantically on the floor.

'*Tabs!*' Sue cried. '*Jerry!* Stop that! What goes on?'

Tabitha had had her differences with her brothers but it was very seldom, particularly in the last year or two, that she had resorted to violence. Her customary method was to assume an aloof superiority which still had the power to enrage and intimidate her more primitive brothers.

Now, however, she was red-faced and bellowing and pounding at Jerry on the floor. The tactics of both would have had them barred from any well-run boxing ring.

Sue pried them apart and discovered that their problem was one of television. Jerry wished to see a puppet show featuring music and comedy. Tabitha preferred a concurrent programme detailing the adventures of a group of young men who were perfectly at home on all the planets – when they weren't battling nameless enemies in outer space. Johnny, meanwhile, was peacefully doing a repeat job of surgery on his horse, most of whose insides were scattered over the rug.

Sue effected a compromise between the two belligerents, and dismissed the matter. After all, company, in a rather

8

isolated community, is exciting, and both the children were probably tired. She was only a little surprised, the next morning, that Tabitha made difficulties about going to school. She loved school and had recently been elected president of her class. Ordinarily she was out in the road long before the bus came. But on this particular day she dawdled and fussed, wriggled while her hair was being plaited, and for breakfast condescended to choke down a spoonful of egg and a half-moon bite of toast.

'What do you suppose is wrong?' Sue exclaimed exhaustedly, when the children had been propelled into the bus.

'Now don't you fret,' Veazie Ann assured her comfortably. 'I've been reading in that book of yours and I guess they'd say she was going through a stage of dis – dis – well, something Eastern.'

'Disorientation,' Sue said, laughing.

'We used to call it cussedness,' Veazie Ann said, 'but it ain't nothing to fret about. You go on back to the hospital, and don't worry.'

Sue almost managed to take her advice. The hospital was a warm hive of activity in which problems were communal, and without the agonizing impact of difficulties in one's personal life.

This week an early snowfall had brought out the skiers, so there were several young men in Denham Two, with legs, arms, and ankles locked in plaster casts. They deplored their misfortunes with great good humour and raced down the corridors in wheel chairs. There was Margot Harrison, too, to claim some of Sue's attention. She still did frequent relief duty on Denham Two and even when she was off duty Sue often encountered her in the Dining Room. The girl seemed to have no happy medium. She was either radiant or crushed, and all conversation led her to her one overwhelming problem.

One day, at dinner, she put her question bluntly. 'Mrs Barry, can I ask you something fresh?'

'It depends on *how* fresh,' Sue said, her eyes twinkling as she buttered her roll.

Margot flushed and said nothing.

'I'm sorry, my dear,' said Sue. 'I didn't mean to make things difficult for you, and I've got a pretty good idea what you want to know. You want to know how I managed to make one intern feel that I was the girl for him.'

'Well,' Margot said, 'that's about it.'

'To tell you the truth,' Sue told her, 'I have no idea. It just sort of grew on us. I didn't even realize that he *was* the one intern for me until I thought he'd given me the heave-ho. *That* brought me up with a jerk.'

'Do you think if I did something like that to Frank . . .?' Margot began hopefully.

'No,' Sue told her honestly, 'I don't. I think Frank would feel very badly for a while, but he'd go on to something else. Bill was, and is, essentially one-track. Frank — well —'

'I know,' Margot said; 'he needs to have his attention focused.' She picked up her tray and sighed wearily. 'Well, maybe something will occur to me. Meanwhile — back to the mines.'

'Wait a minute,' Sue said sharply. 'Margot — doesn't your profession mean a lot to you? You're such a good nurse.'

'I love nursing,' Margot said. 'I'll want to do it all my life. But this is something altogether different. I don't mean to sound conceited, Mrs Barry, but I know perfectly well

I'm not a mud fence, and I know Frank really isn't the only man in the world. But for me – for me –'

'I know,' said Sue gently. She thought of Bill fifty miles away, Bill whom she saw only once a month. 'I hope to tell you I know.'

Frank Warren appeared on the floor that night but his pleasant breezy manner no longer entertained Sue.

I'd like, she thought, to take that young man over my knee. Him and his charm and his brains and his great future! If he doesn't want the girl, why does he play her along?

That night, however, Sue found Veazie Ann waiting up for her, and Margot, Frank, and everything in the hospital left her mind.

'I thought you should know right off,' Veazie Ann said, 'Miss Layton brought Tabitha home from school early.'

'Is she sick?'

'No. Seems she just got to crying and nobody couldn't stop her. Her teacher sent a message along.' She handed Sue a slip of paper.

DEAR MRS BARRY:

Can you come to see me as early tomorrow as is convenient? I feel that it is extremely important that we discuss Tabitha's problems at the first possible opportunity.

Sincerely,
Grace C. Longman

Oh, Lord, Sue thought, then there *is* something to worry about.

12

Young lady with lamp

SUE awoke early the next morning still troubled over Tabitha. A long night of thinking had given her no ease of mind, and she hoped that the visit to Miss Longman, who had had a good deal of experience with children, would provide her with some solution.

She went into the nursery where the baby sat thoughtfully transferring a clothes-pin from one tin cup to another. Sue picked her up and held the warm, firm little body close, remembering wistfully the day when Tabitha had been as uncomplicated.

I wish I could help you as easily now, Tabs darling, she thought.

The ride through the silvery morning raised her spirits somewhat and when she entered the fourth-grade classroom Tabitha greeted her with a radiant smile.

'Mummy!' Tabs called.

Miss Longman rose.

'All right now, everybody,' she said; 'Mrs Barry and I are going into the Teachers' Room to talk. If you need anything *very* badly, you can find me. But I'd like to see all the work papers finished before I come back.'

She motioned Sue through the door, followed her and closed it gently.

'Can you leave them alone like that?' Sue asked, remembering the riots that had started in her childhood the minute Teacher left the room.

'Oh, yes,' said Miss Longman, easily, 'I've had this group for two years and they're adjusted to being responsible. I'm really very proud of their attention span.'

'Oh,' said Sue.

In the Teachers' Room Miss Longman drew two chairs together. She was a good-looking woman, a little younger than Sue with short brown hair and a fair, rosy skin. She was so completely at ease that Sue was forced to remind herself that, in a hospital, Miss Longman would be as out of place and as unfamiliar with the shop talk as Sue was here.

'Tell me, Mrs Barry,' Miss Longman said, 'has Tabitha seemed rather out of sorts lately?'

'She has indeed,' Sue answered fervently.

'We've had quite a little trouble with her here,' Miss Longman said. 'I'm sure that crying spell yesterday was the symptom of some deeply rooted anxiety. She's quite all right physically, I suppose?'

'Oh, yes. She's perfectly healthy, I assure you. And I agree with you about the anxiety. But it's so difficult to make out what's causing it.'

Miss Longman drummed on her chair arm. 'Before I came here,' she said, 'I worked for some years in the Wee School in the Woods just outside New York. We found those symptoms very common in children from broken homes. They –'

'Oh, no, Miss Longman!' Sue interrupted, appalled. '*Tabitha's* home isn't broken! Her father's sick, of course, but I've explained that he's going to get well, and she was perfectly all right about it for weeks. It's only lately that she's been behaving oddly.'

Miss Longman looked thoughtful. 'Mrs Barry,' she said, 'I'll be perfectly frank with you.'

In Sue's experience that always meant that something very disagreeable was coming, and though Miss Longman was obviously a competent and conscientious teacher, Sue was beginning to dislike her.

'I understand about Dr Barry's illness,' Miss Longman said. 'And of course, it's a very disrupting thing to happen to any family.'

She's telling *me* it's disrupting! Sue thought.

'And,' Miss Longman continued, 'when it happened Tabitha undoubtedly turned to you for additional attention. Then – you'll forgive me – you left her too, for your job.'

So *that's* what she's driving at, Sue thought. Tabitha feels deserted both by Bill and me?

A hundred replies sprang to Sue's lips. She could point out that she had breakfast with the children every morning. She could mention her two days a week at home, in which every waking minute was spent with them. She might even mention that she herself was probably a better mother to them than she would have been if she had moped around the house brooding about Bill and the general situation. But she said none of these things, because it was possible – it was entirely possible – that Miss Longman was right.

'I see,' was all Sue remarked.

Miss Longman rose. 'Well, I have to get back,' she said. 'I can trust the class pretty far but after all they're still children. I hope you'll think over what I said, Mrs Barry. And do believe that we all want to help Tabitha in every way we can.'

'Thank you,' Sue answered sincerely. It was evident that Miss Longman meant what she said.

All the way home Sue's thoughts were depressing. *Had*

she sacrificed Tabitha to her own immediate mental comfort? It was all very well to say that she was doing an immeasurable service in the hospital, that good nurses had no right to waste their talent and their training; that she was making a valuable financial contribution to the family – but hadn't she, Sue Barton Barry, always maintained that any mother's first responsibility was to the children she had brought into the world?

'Oh dear,' said Sue aloud, and realized that her voice sounded dreary and confused – as Tabitha's had become lately.

Sue felt a sudden need to talk to someone with a little more formal education than Veazie Ann, so instead of going home she drove across the valley to the hospital and went straight to Kit's office. Kit was alone, but she was frowning over the papers on her desk. When Sue appeared she looked up with relief.

'Oh, thank heaven!' she said. 'I've been dying for somebody to interrupt me. I'm going nuts. Let's go and get a cup of coffee.'

'You're sure you can spare the time?'

'Certainly not! Naturally *you* wouldn't understand how much work this job entails! What's the matter, Bat? You look depressed.'

'You're putting it very mildly indeed.'

In the dining-room Sue explained. 'And the trouble is,' she added, 'that the woman is probably right. You can't open a book or a magazine without reading something that frightens you to death about children's need for security.'

'Well, I suppose it's a point,' Kit answered. 'We have kids come in here scared blue and we have others who are perfectly sure everything is going to be all right. But I don't

know enough about it to advise you. I haven't any children —
I'm just a withered old maid.'

Sue looked at Kit's animated face, her shining red-brown
hair, her alert brown eyes, and grinned. 'You're breaking
my heart,' she said.

'But Bill's not a withered old maid.'

'Well, no, dear,' Sue conceded.

'Then why don't you ask *him* about it? You're going
over tomorrow, aren't you?'

'I don't know,' Sue said doubtfully. 'He'll be looking
forward to a cheerful afternoon. Why should I dump a lot
of domestic troubles in his lap? What kind of a visit does
that make?'

'Oh, for heaven's sake!' Kit said. 'Give the man credit!
Bill isn't the kind who wants to be shut off from life. He'd
like to help, and I'll bet he can. Maybe you don't appreciate
him, but I do.'

'Well, just so you don't let the appreciation run away
with you . . .' Sue murmured.

Later, however, she perceived that Kit was right. It
wasn't fair to shut Bill away from his family, trouble or
no, and he would be a big help. He was good with people in
general and his tie with Tabitha was very close. The next
day she gave him a long and detailed account of the entire
situation, including her talk with Miss Longman.

'Well,' Bill said thoughtfully, 'it's the obvious explanation. Nine out of ten people would agree with Miss Longman.'

'Then you think I ought to leave the hospital?'

'No,' said Bill, 'not just yet. Somehow it doesn't seem
like Tabs, wanting to be babied, yammering for Mama.
She's generally the one who wants to look out for people,

and she's got a lot of spunk. Even if she did miss us more than we think, I don't believe she'd carry on like that about it. I think there's a good chance that there's something else that's bothering her. Why not at least try to figure it out on that basis?'

'You could be right,' Sue admitted. 'Anyway, I'll do my best. And if I can't find anything else wrong, after a reasonable length of time, I'll just assume that Miss Longman is right and I'll stay at home.'

'Good! Now tell me about the rest of the outfit. Any new Cute Sayings we can send to the newspapers?'

As she drove home Sue became more and more convinced that Bill's hunch was the right one. Tabitha was troubled by something more subtle than a mere need for her parents' constant presence. But what on earth was it? She wasn't jealous of the baby; she got along well with her brothers, and until the fit of being out of joint with the world had overtaken her she had been doing very well at school. If it weren't any of these things – what on earth was it?

She was still puzzling over it as she turned into the driveway, and she was surprised to see the front door open to the icy mountain air, and Veazie Ann standing there waving to her.

'*Sue!*' Veazie Ann called, 'I've been watching for you. Go right over to the Stuarts. Cal's cut herself! And your bag's over there!'

Sue swung the car around without pausing for questions, forgetting Tabitha's problem for the moment in her sympathy for Cal. Even if the cut was not serious, Cal would be in a difficult situation. Mona Stuart was admittedly helpless in the presence of domestic crises. The difference between the world in which she painted and the world around her was too great to permit her to be of much use in the latter. And Cornelia, the maid, ordinarily a pillar of strength, became faint at the sight of blood! Sue pressed her foot down an the accelerator.

She opened the door without knocking and found Cal on the living-room sofa, looking a little white, but smiling, and holding a tourniquet tightly twisted about her arm. Her mother stood at the end of the couch, looking dumpy and rather pathetic. The most astonishing occupant of the room was Sue's own daughter, busily wiping the blood from Cal's arm with a towel.

'Cal!' Sue exclaimed. 'What happened? Tabs, what are *you* doing here?'

Cal grinned. 'I got too smart trying to sharpen my own skates,' she said, 'but I'm all right now, thanks to Tabs.'

'Here's your bag, Mummy,' said Tabitha importantly.

Sue removed the tourniquet, looked at the cut briefly and said it might need a stitch.

'I've called Dr Mason,' Mrs Stuart said. 'He'll get here as soon as he can. Cal seemed to be bleeding quite badly, and I'm just no good at this sort of thing. I was scared to death when I found you weren't home.'

'But *I* was home,' Tabitha said, 'and I came right over with your bag, in case Cal needed something in it. There was a tourniquet, so we put it on.'

'*She* put it on, Mrs Barry,' Cal said. 'I was going to tell her what to do, but she knew without.'

'Of course I did,' Tabitha said. 'I had just the same thing when *I* was young, only it was my leg and *much* worse. Mummy put a tourniquet on it and I've been practising ever since.'

'Why, Tabs!' said Sue, 'you never put one on a *person* — just on your dolls.'

'But I knew *how*!' said Tabitha, 'and there wasn't any person to put one on until just now. You know, Mummy' — her voice grew a little cold — 'I can really do lots of things you don't seem to know about.'

Sue removed the tourniquet again and applied a pressure bandage which would keep Cal more comfortable until the doctor came, but from time to time she glanced up at her daughter.

Tabs looked such a *little* girl, her brown snow pants pulled over her green gingham school dress, her black braid swinging against her shoulders. Why, she was just a *baby*!

And yet, Sue was forced to admit, this afternoon she had acted far more coolly and intelligently than a great many adults, including Cal's mother.

'That was swell of you, Tabs,' she said.

Tabs flushed. 'Well, of course, Cal had to tell me *where* to put it,' she said.

'But that was all I had to tell her,' Cal interrupted. 'I was so rattled I wouldn't even have thought if she hadn't asked me whether it was bleeding from a vein or an artery.'

Mona Stuart suddenly echoed Sue's thoughts. 'Even allowing for her background,' she said, 'I think that was a remarkable performance, Sue. I'm darned grateful to Tabs.'

'Oh, it wasn't anything,' said Tabitha airily.

Dr Mason's car pulled up at the door, and after examining the cut he agreed that it needed a stitch. Both Cal and her mother assured Sue that they could manage without her and Sue promised to look in later in the evening to see if there were anything she could do to make Cal comfortable.

It was on the way home that Sue noticed the change in

Tabitha's expression. The child's face seemed fuller and her mouth had lost the slight downward turn it had taken in the past few weeks.

'Tabs,' said Sue quietly, 'I'm proud of you.'

To her astonishment Tabs did not respond to this praise. On the contrary she was silent until they had stopped in their own garage, and then, before Sue had a chance to open the door, she put her hand on her mother's arm. Her voice was desperately earnest.

'The trouble is, Mummy,' she said, 'what *nobody* seems to understand, is that I *can* do *real* things. I did them today and I could do a lot more, especially if you'd teach me how.'

It was as though the dial on a combination safe had suddenly been turned to the right numbers. So *that* was what was wrong with Tabs! She was past the little-girl stage of wanting patronizing adult praise. She wanted to do *real* things, things which gave her the importance which she felt was due to her. But it had to be the genuine article. Sue looked at her daughter with the beginning of the respect one adult might feel for another. Tabs was no fool, and there was nothing phony about her.

'Darling,' said Sue, 'I'll teach you everything I can, all the things you're able to learn.'

'Thank you, Mummy,' was all that Tabitha said, but she rested her cheek against Sue's arm. She looked composed and happy, as though an ugly wrinkle had been smoothed away.

Sue smiled down with tenderness at the dark head; but when they came into the house, Sue picked up her youngest out of the high chair and kissed the fragrant red curls. She was glad that there was still a baby in the house.

13

Mistletoe

'I'M terribly sorry, Mrs Barry,' Miss Patton said, her pencil poised over the time sheet.

'Don't worry,' said the disappointed Sue. 'Those things happen. It's perfectly all right.'

'But it *isn't* all right,' Miss Patton said unhappily. 'Nurses who have children ought to have Christmas Eve off. I had you down for it – but with *two* of the day shift sick, I simply can't cover the relief. Anyway,' she added hopefully, 'you'll have Christmas Day off. That ought to help.'

'It's swell,' Sue assured her. 'Who's on with me?'

'Mrs Glennon, and – let's see – Eben is off, and Peggy. . . . You'll have George, and Margot Harrison comes on seven to eleven. But you ought to have an easy night, the floor census is always way down at Christmas.'

Sue accepted the change philosophically, though it meant rearranging all her plans at home, and she did not look forward to coming in at midnight, trimming a large Christmas tree, and getting into bed around three in the morning, only to be awakened at six by her exuberant family.

Veazie Ann made short work of the problem.

'Shucks!' she said. 'You ain't a-going to do no such a thing. I was trimming Christmas trees afore you was born. Soon's I get the kids to bed, I'll start in. It'll be done afore you get home. Jest put the tree presents in one pile, and the stocking presents in another, so's I'll know.'

'But you were going to church,' Sue protested. 'And you still could. After all, Cal would baby-sit for you.'

'The church'll still be there, come Christmas morning. I ain't going to argue, Sue. I'm a-doing it.'

'Well . . .' said Sue weakly. 'But Veazie Ann, leave the stockings for me, will you? I can't bear not to do *some* of it.'

The matter rested at that.

Meanwhile, in the hospital the floors were beginning to take on a green and festive look. The glass-walled Nurses' Rooms were embellished with Christmas scenes cut from coloured paper, over which hung motionless white cotton snowflakes. Christmas cards from ex-patients covered all available door space. Wreaths of holly or ground pine hung at the windows and the air began to have a woodsy smell.

As many patients as possible went home in the week before Christmas. Those who remained on Denham Two were cheerful and interested, for many of them were older men whose children were grown up and married, or whose wives were dead. These found Christmas at the hospital far more cheering than Christmas with a married son or daughter. Here they had an importance, were part of the general festivities and were happy.

One patient, in fact, who had been discharged a month before, contrived to get himself back into the hospital for Christmas. A bad heart case, long separated from his wife, and living alone, he had loved being in hospital; had enjoyed the routine, the jokes with the nurses, the feeling of comfort and security; and he had made friends with all the long-term patients. He had gone home protesting, but his good-bye to the nurses had been a cheerful, 'I'll be back for Christmas, girls!'

They had thought he was joking – but he was not and he returned to the hospital by the simple expedient of running up the hospital hill. He was brought back to Denham Two on a stretcher, gasping and blue, and with a broad grin.

'Here I am,' he panted to Sue. 'I told you! Now I'll have to stay all winter.'

The twenty-fourth of December can hardly be said to have dawned. It emerged, slowly, into a smother of snow, but the ploughs were out and when Sue left for the hospital at a quarter past two she found the road clear and sanded.

At least, she thought, we'll have a gorgeous white Christmas, which will be lovely for the children.

Denham Two was warm, comfortable, and cheerful, and Sue felt that if she could not be at home it was good to be here. Everybody greeted her with 'Merry Christmas!' The nurses' desk was piled with boxes of candy. A huge, three-layer, home-made frosted cake, the gift of a grateful patient's wife, stood in elegant solitude on the shelf under the medicine cabinet. A bunch of mistletoe hung over the doorway.

Miss Patton was not tired today, nor rumpled. 'We have only seventeen patients,' she announced, 'and four of them are specialed. If there aren't any accidents you won't have enough to do to keep you awake.'

'I can bear up,' said Pat dryly.

The work was, in fact, ridiculously easy, compared to most evenings. 'And you deserve it,' the relief supervisor told them. 'Take it easy while you can.'

Even the Nurses' Dining Room was unusually festive, with decorations, white tablecloths, candlelight, and a buffet supper.

Margot Harrison came on duty at seven o'clock looking very young and pretty – but not very happy, and in this she was undoubtedly justified, for everybody knew that Frank Warren was dating other girls now as much as he dated Margot. Particularly he dated the tiny, self-possessed Nancy Littlefield, whose short, curly blonde hair reminded Sue of a dandelion puff which had managed to retain its gold. Nancy, however, was not unduly impressed by Frank, or by any of the other young men who so earnestly pursued her; and in this, Sue thought sadly, Nancy rather had the edge on Margot.

Just when it was that Margot first noticed the mistletoe over the office doorway Sue didn't know, but she saw that Margot's glance strayed to it often, each time with brighter eyes. What was going on in the girl's mind, in view of the fact that Frank Warren was on duty that night, was obvious.

Sue smiled at the youngness of it and then thought, Oh, dear! I hope she isn't going to work this up into a matter of life and death. If she starts thinking that whether he does or doesn't kiss her under the mistletoe is going to Mean Something . . .

Sue remembered the days when she, herself, had done just that sort of thing. *If* a green bus came up Market Street first, instead of a yellow one, she would pass her history test; *if* her mother had pancakes for breakfast instead of oatmeal, Phil Macdonal would walk home from school with her.

Sue hoped, suddenly, that Frank Warren would somehow be prevented from coming to Denham Two that night,

and for a while it seemed that he had been, for just as the
dietitian came up on the floor to serve the supper trays the
hospital loudspeaker buzzed and said breathily: *Dr Warren! Dr Frank Warren!*

A little later the office telephone rang and Sue answered
it.

'Is Dr Warren there?' the operator asked.

'No, he isn't.'

'Well, he hasn't answered the page. If he comes through
will you have him call the Operating Room? Dr Mackin
has a ruptured appendix on the way in, and you know,
Mrs Barry, he's going to have a fit if Dr Warren isn't
ready.'

'I know. I'll tell Dr Warren if I see him.'

'Thanks. Merry Christmas, Mrs Barry.'

'Same to you, Gertie.'

There was a click, and then the loudspeaker began again,
Dr WarREN. Dr Frank W ARren!

'Trays are ready,' the dietitian announced firmly through
the office window, and Sue had no time to meditate on the
idea that she hadn't wanted *anybody* to have a ruptured
appendix in order to keep Frank Warren off the floor,
especially on Christmas Eve.

The trays were bright with Christmas mats and napkins;
the supper was good; and as more and more visitors appeared laden with Christmas packages, the patients became
hilarious. Denham Two buzzed with good cheer and Sue
was amused to find herself wondering how anyone could
think a hospital dreary.

It was at a quarter to eight, without warning that the
corridor lights went out – were put out, in fact, by Sue, in
response to the telephone operator's request that she do so.
'Up' patients and visitors collected in doorways and peered

inquiringly in all directions, uncertain as to whether this sudden darkness was accidental or intentional.

There was a brief pause, and then '*Adeste Fideles*' rang down the corridor as two by two a choir of student nurses emerged from the gloom, their young faces lighted against wavering darkness by candles in the Florence Nightingale lamps they carried. The soft glow shone on their starched bibs and collars and made their eyes enormous and brilliant beneath the white flare of their caps.

They looked heartbreakingly young, in those caps, in the night, but their fresh sweet voices came clear and strong as they paced in a slow, candle-lit procession down the corridor to its end and back again, singing now, 'It Came Upon a Midnight Clear,' and then, 'Silent Night, Holy Night.'

When they were gone there was a silence, and then, as Pat switched the lights on, Sue beheld a huge man who was convalescing from pneumonia, standing in the door of his room, shamelessly wiping his eyes on his bathrobe sleeve.

'Them s-sweet young kids,' he said helplessly, and Sue understood exactly how he felt.

It was some time later, when the last over-stimulated patient had been settled for the night, and the last sleeping pill had been doled out, that Sue and Pat found themselves sitting in the office in actual idleness. Margot leaned in the doorway, and George sat in Eben's place on the stretcher in the corridor, swinging his legs.

'Heavenly Day!' Pat exclaimed suddenly. 'Mr Mills's dressing! It'll have to be done. I forgot all about it!'

'That's the trouble with an easy night,' said Sue. 'You forget things a lot more easily than you do when things are rushed.'

'I'll do the dressing, Mrs Glennon,' Margot said from the doorway. 'I'd be glad to have something to do.'

'All right,' Pat agreed. 'But don't bother with the dressing cart at this time of night. It makes such a racket. Just take a clean binder and one of the small cans of sterile gauze.'

Margot hurried away down the once more darkened corridor and Pat was just beginning, 'I remember, once, in my hospital at Christmas –' when she was interrupted by the sound of quick steps and a starchy rustle. The next instant Nancy Littlefield whirled briskly into the office looking very trim and asked, 'Mrs Glennon, could I borrow some potassium permanganate crystals?'

'Sure, if we have any. Look in the glass cabinet in the Utility Room, middle shelf.'

Nancy vanished and Pat said idly, 'Pretty kid.'

'Yes,' Sue answered, 'but –'

'But not your favourite for the Warren sweepstakes. Well, I'm on your side, but little Harrison is too anxious.'

'My dear girl,' said Sue, 'have you ever been in love?'

'I still am,' Pat admitted, 'but the beginning was a long time ago. Come to think of it, I guess I was anxious, too.'

They were prevented from sharing reminiscences by the sudden appearance of a tall, lank figure whose large hands scooped half a layer of chocolates from the open box on the desk. 'Hiyah, babes!' said Frank Warren cheerfully, pulling out a chair. He folded up on it, filled his mouth with candy, and then, speechless, picked a chart out of the rack and began to write progress notes. He was still engrossed when Nancy Littlefield returned to the office.

'Thank you very much, Mrs Glennon,' she said. 'I don't know how we happened to be short, especially on Denham Three.'

Frank Warren looked up at her, grinned, and went on writing.

Nancy grinned back and turned to leave when she saw the mistletoe and halted. 'Hm,' she said and winked at Pat. 'Er – would you have a stool handy, Mrs Glennon?'

'There's one in the linen closet,' said Pat, poker-faced.

Nancy placed the stool carefully in the doorway under the mistletoe, climbed up on it, and stood waiting, while Sue and Pat exchanged amused glances. Then, as nothing happened, Nancy said firmly, 'Well, Dr Warren, nobody can say I'm not making it easy for you.'

He swung around in his chair, bewildered but cheerful. 'Do something for you?' he asked.

'You certainly can!'

Warren looked at Pat, who pointed wordlessly to the mistletoe.

'Oh!' he said. 'Why, honey-chile!' He unfolded his long length from the chair, found his head on a level with Nancy's, clasped her melodramatically in his arms and kissed her – warmly.

'That's for Christmas,' he said. 'And for good measure, here's another, in case we're both dead by New Year.'

Nancy emerged slightly rumpled from his embrace, said demurely, 'Thank you kindly, sir,' picked up the stool, re-placed it in the linen closet, and went on her way, laughing.

'Nice evening,' said Dr Warren comfortably; scooped up another handful of chocolates, and returned to his chart.

Sue was the only one who had seen Margot Harrison come down the corridor just as Frank had kissed Nancy the second time. She had halted, frozen, until Nancy stooped to retrieve the stool.

Then she fled.

14

New Year's Eve

Sue was distressed about Margot, but she had no time to worry about her, for the next day was Christmas. She was at home with the children all the morning, and she spent the afternoon with Bill. By the time she returned to duty, she found Margot busy and apparently cheerful, though with very little to say.

In the dining-room, on several occasions, Sue heard a few rumours to the effect that Margot Harrison seemed to be giving young Warren 'a brush-off', and that His Highness wasn't liking it. A hospital dining-room, however, is always full of rumours which grow wilder by the hour, and aside from hoping that these were true, Sue gave the matter very little thought. After all, it was Margot's business; she had not asked Sue for any advice nor offered any confidences. Better let the child run her own affairs.

The hospital, between Christmas and New Year, remained half empty as usual, for only emergencies were willing to come in during the holidays, and the emergencies, poor things, had no choice. So the work was light, and by the end of the week Sue was beginning to feel bored. So, perhaps, was everyone else. A hospital staff, accustomed to working at top speed, begins to develop an excess of energy after a week of comparative idleness – an energy which is likely to find an outlet in various ways – from violent attacks of cleaning and scrubbing to sporadic outbursts of general nonsense.

On the last day of December, when Sue came on duty, she heard laughter in the Emergency Room as she passed it, and more in the Nurses' Room on Denham Two.

'What goes on?' she demanded as she hung up her coat and her cap.

The day nurses crowding the room looked at her joyfully. 'You mean you haven't heard about Warren and Miss Bagley?'

Miss Bagley was supervisor of the big women's ward in the main building, an austere nurse not given to smiling. Sue had heard that Miss Bagley regarded Frank Warren as 'a nice boy', but that was all she had heard. The day shift enlightened her as to the change.

Frank Warren had persuaded the Emergency Room nurses to bandage his head, leaving only one eye visible. He had then settled himself on a stretcher, covered himself with a sheet, and one of the ambulance drivers had solemnly wheeled him to the entrance to Ward A. Frank's groans were described as horrible, and the maddened Miss Bagley had protested in vain that it was all a mistake – that she could not, and would not, have a *man* in there. When she had argued herself frantic, and had rushed to the telephone to settle the matter, Frank, with a final bellow, had sat up, swept the bandage from his head, and burst into roars of laughter. Miss Bagley had laughed, but she was good and sore all the same.

'I don't blame her,' said Pat, who was standing at Sue's elbow. 'That ward is enough of a madhouse, without little boys making it worse. I'm glad it wasn't *here*. I'd have killed him. A cut-up, yet!'

'Oh, come on, Mrs Glennon,' the younger nurses

protested, but Pat, though laughing, stuck to her point.

Frank's jokes, however, seemed to have released a general flood of idiocy. Even the staid Eben was affected, for when Sue, pouring out a four o'clock ounce of whisky for a very old patient, said that the ward bottle was getting low, and had Eben been tippling on the sly, Eben only grinned.

He was a rabid teetotaller, given to announcing from time to time, that nobody had ever smelled whisky on *him*, and nobody ever would.

Now he said nothing; but a little later, when Sue went into the linen closet for a towel, Eben quietly but happily closed the door and locked her in. As Pat was giving medicines and Peggy was taking temperatures, it was some time before Sue got out.

'You rat!' she told Eben, laughing. 'I'll fix you! Just wait and see!'

Eben fled in mock terror, and Pat said, 'I know what'll do it!'

'What?'

'*You* wait and see.'

Sue waited, and presently Eben reappeared and stood leaning against the stretcher in the hall, talking to young Ezra Prouty, who was an 'up' patient.

It was then that Pat came innocently along the corridor carrying something concealed in one hand. She passed close to Eben and raised her hand casually.

Eben yelled, Ezra Prouty doubled up with joy, and Pat returned demurely and without haste to the office, remarking over her shoulder, '*That'll* teach you to lock nurses in the linen closet!'

'What *did* you do?' Sue demanded.

'Oh, I just dumped a thimbleful of whisky on the lapel

of his coat.' She opened her hand, revealing a small test tube.

Sue shouted with laughter, stepped out into the corridor and said, 'Phew! Frightful smell around here.'

Eben looked foolish. Ezra doubled up again, and hurried to inform every patient on the floor. They, in turn, conspicuously held their noses whenever Eben appeared.

'Wow!' they said loudly. 'Thought you didn't drink, Eben. Oh, boy! What a breath!'

' *'Tain't* my breath!' Eben spluttered. 'Those dratted nurses –'

Once Sue, meeting Eben in the corridor, smiled broadly and sniffed. Eben returned the smile almost too promptly and said, 'Him that laughs last laughs best.'

These mild antics, meanwhile, had set young Ezra Prouty thinking. He had come in with a mild bronchial pneumonia, had been out of bed for several days, and was going home shortly. In the interim, he kept himself most usefully busy around the floor, waiting on the other patients, carrying trays back to the kitchen, filling icecaps, and doing innumerable small jobs for the nurses. At supper-time, he lurked in the vicinity of the kitchen, for the dietitian was young and very pretty, and Ezra was seldom far away when she was there.

Tonight was no exception, and when the patients had finished supper. Ezra was assiduous in carrying back trays. The nurses were not aware of anything unusual until Miss Roxey appeared in the office, white and breathless.

'Help!' she said. 'I guess I'm in a terrible mess, girls.'

'Why?' said Pat, instantly concerned.

'Well, I – it seems – Mr Bienvenue got a regular diet on his tray, and he ate every bit of it! Dr Mackin will have my

head, and goodness only knows what it'll do to Mr Bienvenue. You'd better call an intern – quick!'

Mr Bienvenue had had a serious stomach operation a
week before, and was still only allowed a few swallows of
broth, tea, or milk, receiving his fluids by infusion.

'I took his tray in,' said Sue slowly. 'He did *not* have
any regular diet.'

'But he *says* he did. He says himself that he ate every
bit – ham, baked potato, string beans, and goodness knows
what else. I *saw* the potato skins – what were left.'

'How did you find out?' Pat wanted to know.

'Ezra told me. He brought the tray back. It had Mr
Bienvenue's name card right on it. Ezra didn't know. He
just came in with the tray, planked it down, and said Mr
Bienvenue wanted to say thanks for the wonderful dinner.
He hadn't expected anything like that for a long time, yet.'

'So *Ezra* told you,' Sue remarked. 'So Ezra didn't know.
That's *very* interesting. And where is Ezra's tray?'

'Why – why, I suppose it's in the kitchen. I didn't notice
when he brought it back. I –' Her eyes widened. 'You
don't mean . . .!' She turned and dashed back to the
kitchen.

Pat and Sue hurried after her. Ezra, surprisingly – had
vanished, but his tray had not, for the kitchenmaid was
just starting to clear off the dishes. There, on the cart, was
Ezra's name card – on a very small tray holding the remains of a cup of broth.

Miss Roxey stared at it, bewildered. 'But *he* said *himself* –
why that miserable wretch! Ezra put him up to saying
that! Where *is* Ezra! Just let me at him!'

Ezra was not to be found, but Mr Bienvenue was unable
to escape. He smiled charmingly at the furious – and greatly
relieved – dietitian.

'It was leetle joke,' he explained. 'Ezra he say he wants to play leetle joke on very pretty girl he like so much. He wants I should just say – sure I eat so beautiful beeg dinner.'

'Well,' Pat said to the crimson dietitian, 'I guess you take it – from this point. Let's hope nobody else feels funny tonight. I'm getting worn out.'

This forlorn wish seemed likely, for a time, to be granted, for the floor settled down to a state of increasing quiet. Backs were uneventfully rubbed, medicines were given for the last time, the corridor lights were put out. New Year's Eve or not, all was calm on Denham Two – until a quarter to ten, when Peggy appeared suddenly, her eyes enormous.

'Mrs Glennon,' she quavered, 'there – there's somebody or – or – something – in Room 4!'

'Nonsense!' Pat said briskly. 'This crazy house is getting you down. Room 4 has been empty for a week.'

'But I *heard* Something, moaning, in there!'

'Oh, mercy!' said Pat, exasperated. Still, a hospital was a hospital, and almost anything could happen in it. Patients had been known to stray.

Room 4 was in plain sight from the office, its door slightly ajar. Pat got up and went across the corridor, pushed open the door, switched on the lights, looked in the bathroom, and came out again. 'There's nothing there,' she said, and returned to the office.

Three minutes later both Sue and Pat leaped in their chairs as a hideous, bloodcurdling moan came unmistakably from Room 4.

'I – I told you!' wailed Peggy, who had remained firmly in the brightly lighted office.

'Come on, Sue,' said Pat, looking slightly green, and together they approached the half-open door.

The room was empty.

'Well –' said Pat helplessly.

The next moan came about ten minutes later, transfixing both nurses. Peggy gave a faint yelp, and all three stared in horror as the door to Room 4 began to swing open – slowly – *very* slowly – and a beaming Eben emerged.

Sue's breath exploded in a gasp. Then all three burst out laughing, a little hysterically.

'Eben,' Pat said, 'if one more thing happens tonight I'm going home, whether it's time or not.'

Eben grinned. 'Pretty good, wasn't I?'

'Humph! Where were you the first time I looked?'

'In the next room.'

'But where were you the second time?'

'In the bathroom. I knew you wouldn't look there twice, and you didn't!'

'Where's your coat?' Peggy found her voice at last.

'Oh, that? It's over there on the stretcher. Didn't think I was going to give myself away with the smell of whisky, did you? And I guess that makes us even,' he added with a broad grin.

At eleven o'clock, the quiet having had no further interruptions, Sue put on her coat and muffler, said good night to everybody, and carrying next day's X-ray slips to be left in the box outside the X-ray rooms, she departed.

As she deposited the slips, however, she noticed a light on in Kit's office. This was so unusual that she wondered, and hurried down the corridor.

Kit looked up wearily from her desk. 'Hi,' she said.

'What on earth are you doing, working at this hour?'

'Oh, just catching up,' Kit said. 'You off, tomorrow?'

'No. Are you?'

'I am, thank goodness. How's about I should come home with you tonight?'

'I'd love it! Put those things away and come on.'

'It'll take me a few minutes. Why don't you go down to the dining-room and have some coffee? I'll be along in a minute or two, and we'll go.'

'Good idea. Want any coffee?'

'Nope. Just had some.'

Sue went on to the dining-room, took her coffee to an empty table near the door, and sat down.

There was a sprinkling of students who had obviously been to the movies, Margot Harrison among them, a further sprinkling of hungry relief nurses just off duty, and two interns at the doctors' table.

Frank Warren was one of the interns, and Sue noticed with interest that though his eyes strayed constantly to Margot, she did not look at him at all.

Good girl, Sue thought, and just then Margot Harrison rose, picked up her plate and coffee cup and started across the room. She was wearing a smartly cut, wine-coloured wool dress; and she looked, Sue thought, particularly pretty.

'Hey, baby,' Frank Warren's voice boomed. 'Where you going?'

'To the Nurses' Home,' said Margot with dignity and continued on her way.

Frank winked at the interested student nurses, rose quickly from the table and came up behind Margot without making a sound. He waited until she had pushed her dishes through the window to the kitchen. Then, before she had time to realize what he was about, he picked her up, slung her over his shoulder regardless of her squeak of dismay, and began to caper, chanting, 'I'm a cave man! I'm a cave man!' while Margot's small fists beat a futile tattoo on his shoulders.

It was at that moment that Kit walked into the dining-room, and, in the dead hush that followed, each word she spoke had a precise and dreadful finality.

'I will see you in my office in fifteen minutes, Miss Harrison.'

15

Miss Van Dyke's position

NOBODY moved or spoke until Kit had turned on her heel and left the dining-room. Then Sue sprang up. She had realized suddenly that she was the only graduate nurse in the room and that, as such, her opinion as an eyewitness would be expected to carry some weight, regardless of her known friendship with Kit.

'It wasn't your fault,' she said to the stricken Margot, who was standing where Frank had hastily put her down. 'I'll explain to Miss Van Dyke.' She added, to the equally stricken Frank, 'You irresponsible young idiot! You've got her in a fine mess!'

Sue swept grandly from the dining-room and caught up with Kit in the hospital lobby. Together they walked slowly back to the Director's Office and paused in the doorway.

'You'd better let me brief you,' said Sue, and told Kit exactly what happened.

'Oh, brother! What a headache!' Kit said. 'That infernal boy and his propensity for fun and games! And why did it have to be Harrison? She's a nice girl and a first-class nurse, and her record has always been splendid.'

'What are you going to do about her?'

Sue didn't ask why Kit was going to do *anything* about Margot, when the situation was manifestly not Margot's fault. Sue had been a Director of Nurses herself, and knew only too well that, if this episode were not made important, the always present sprinkling of irresponsible students who are to be found in any school would soon be romping all over the place.

'After all,' Kit said, continuing Sue's thought, 'High Jinks in the Hospital, among doctors and nurses, however extenuating the circumstances, doesn't tend, somehow, to give the general public that feeling of confidence and security that they ought to have. And these things get out, especially in a small community. I'll have to campus her, at least, but I'll see that it doesn't go on her permanent record. It's unfair to Harrison, but to do nothing would be worse, and you know it.'

'Yes,' Sue agreed, and then, seized with a sudden inspiration, she said, 'As a matter of fact, you're in a position to do quite a bit *for* Harrison.'

'You mean she'll love being restricted for something that isn't her fault?'

'No' – seriously. 'I mean, she's frantically in love with Warren.'

'Poor kid! Well, this ought to teach her.'

'But *I* think he's in love with *her*. He just hasn't discovered it yet. She told me herself, once, that he needed his attention focused. He's too scattered. That's where you come in.'

'Not me!' said Kit emphatically. 'Even if I were running a Lonely Hearts Club, instead of a nursing school, I still wouldn't wish that lightweight on a nice kid like Harrison.'

'I don't think he *is* a lightweight, and I'll bet he shows up here any minute, to take all the blame.'

'Well, what does that prove? *I* can't do anything to *him*. He'll apologize, and explain – and Margot still takes the rap.'

'You can do something,' Sue insisted. 'You can give

him a good scare. Make him think you're going to expel Margot. That ought to get him focused on her.'

'Well,' said Kit doubtfully, moving into the office and settling at her desk, 'I don't like meddling in people's lives.'

Sue remained standing. 'You wouldn't be meddling,' she protested. 'There's no reason why he shouldn't take *some* of the consequences of his own behaviour. But you'll have to sound awfully stuffy. He's no fool.'

Kit considered for a moment. Then she grinned. 'All right,' she said. 'He's probably rattled just now. I'll give him the idea that I think Margot is fast, and man-crazy, and a disgrace to her profession, and that I'm going to send her packing. He'd see through that, if he had time to think – but he hasn't.'

She broke off as steps came rapidly along the corridor. A moment later Frank Warren appeared, to stand sheepishly in the doorway.

'Look, Miss Van Dyke,' he began, gesturing awkwardly, 'I – Oh, don't go, Mrs Barry – you were there, you can bear me out. Miss Van Dyke, what happened in the dining-room was entirely my fault. Honest. Margot didn't even know I was there until I grabbed her.'

'That's gentlemanly of you, Dr Warren,' Kit said pompously. 'Most gentlemanly. But I'm afraid that I can't regard Miss Harrison's conduct as anything but inexcusable.'

'It wasn't *her* conduct,' Frank said desperately. 'It was *mine*!' He turned to Sue. 'Mrs Barry – you saw the whole thing.'

'Mrs Barry has told me the facts as she sincerely believes them to be,' Kit said, her stuffiness growing by leaps and bounds. 'Nevertheless, it is entirely evident that there is more behind it. No girl provokes attention of that kind, unless she means to.'

Sue choked slightly. She hoped Kit wasn't overdoing this.

'You must understand my position, Dr Warren,' Kit went on stonily. 'We cannot have behaviour of this sort in the hospital. A diploma from this school is respected. We can't have our standards lowered by such antics.'

Sue's face ached with her effort to keep it serious and unsmiling. This was too corny a caricature to fool anybody. Surely Frank must see through it.

But he didn't. He stared at Kit with loathing and his attitude changed abruptly from shamefaced apology to anger.

'No, I *don't* understand your position, Miss Van Dyke. I don't understand it at all. It's ridiculous! Do you mean to say that you would actually ruin that nice kid's whole career because of a little foolish horseplay?' He paused, struck by sudden horror. 'Hey,' he said. 'You – you're implying that Margot *isn't* a nice girl – that she isn't a – a – *lady*!'

Sue looked at him with interest. Wow! she thought. Kitty is really getting into him.

'*I* should say,' Kit was replying, 'that your conduct implied the same thing.'

'I implied nothing of the sort,' the boy said furiously, and his young anger did Sue's heart good. 'She – she's a fine girl – and a splendid nurse – and if you can't see –'

'I see that you did your utmost to disprove that,' Kit began, and broke off suddenly as Margot appeared in the doorway. 'Oh! Miss Harrison. Will you wait just a few minutes in the Nursing School Office? I'll call you when I'm ready to see you.'

Sue looked at Margot's piteously white face and – winked.

Margot stared, brightened, and quickly assumed a mask-like expression. But she went away with light steps and Sue relaxed.

'The whole thing is lousy!' Frank was raging 'And I'm not going to leave it at that. If you fire that kid I'll take it to the Board of Directors. I – I'll resign! There are other hospitals – and maybe some of them have heard that we're living in the twentieth century!'

At this point both Sue and Kit were seized with a fit of coughing.

'Well, Dr Warren,' Kit said when she had recovered, 'I must consider. Your sincerity has impressed me and I am beginning to feel that your relationship with Miss Harrison is not as cheap as this episode led me to believe.'

'*Cheap!*' Warren roared. '*Cheap!* For Pete's sake! That's the girl I'm going to marry! That's how cheap it is –' He broke off, his face ludicrous with shock as he realized what he had said. He remained for a moment startled and uncertain; then he straightened and his gestures lost their clumsiness. He planked a huge, decisive fist on Kit's desk. 'That's right,' he said. 'I sure *am* going to marry her – if she'll have me.'

Kit and Sue looked at him, momentarily paralysed. They had hardly expected this.

'I think,' said Kit, finding her voice at last, 'that you might ask Miss Harrison to come in now, Mrs Barry.'

Sue found Margot anxious and still shaken, despite Sue's wink. 'Everything's swell,' Sue told her. 'Don't worry for a minute.'

'Oh, Mrs Barry. You did this. How can I ever –'

'I did nothing of the sort. Frank did it.'

'Frank? What –'

'Never mind. Come on!' And together they went into Kit's awful Presence.

'Miss Harrison,' Kit said, 'I understand from Dr Warren that this disgraceful performance is not entirely your fault –'

'I've been telling you –' Frank began, in a tone so violently masterful that Margot looked at him in astonishment – and pride.

'In view of the circumstances,' Kit went on, ignoring Frank, 'I have decided to limit your punishment to two weeks restricted to campus – and may I offer you my congratulations?'

'Wh-what?' said Margot.

'Oh, for Pete's sake,' Frank said exasperated. 'I told Miss Van Dyke that you're the girl I want to marry – but I didn't explain I hadn't asked you yet. Will –'

'I think,' said Kit firmly, 'that it's time Miss Harrison got back to her dormitory. Will you see her over, Dr Warren?'

'I – uh – er – *I sure will*! Come on, kid! Oh, and Miss Van Dyke – forgive me for getting sore. You're a pretty good egg at that.'

'Thank you,' Kit replied demurely.

It was not until the last sound of two pairs of footsteps had died away down the long corridor that Kit and Sue dissolved into helpless laughter.

16

St Valentine's Day

THAT first day of February was unusually dreary and the jonquils on Kit's desk seemed the only cheering note in the universe – until the telephone rang.

Kit picked up the receiver and said automatically, 'Miss Van Dyke.'

'Hiyah, Kitten,' said a masculine voice.

Kit's face lighted. 'Bill! For heaven's sake! Where are you?'

'Indian Stream, but not for much longer. I'm coming home the fourteenth. I'm cured, Toots!'

'Oh, Bill, I'm so glad! Does Sue know?'

'Nope. And you're not going to tell her. I'm a Valentine's Day surprise. That's why I called you.'

'I'm right with you. What do you want me to do? Wrap you up in paper lace?'

'That won't be necessary. Just see that Sue is off the fourteenth and fifteenth, that's all.'

'It's done. But how are you getting over? I'd be glad to come and get you.'

'Thanks – but skip it. I'd rather you'd take the day off to keep my girl home until I get there.'

'Ouch!' said Kit, and listened with pleasure to Bill's laughter, for they both knew about Sue and her energy.

'But look,' Kit said, 'are you *really* all right?'

'Sure. Clean bill of health. I'll have to stick around home

for another month, but after that I'll be back on the job.'

'Well, it's a darned good thing you told me, because Sue will quit here the minute she knows, and she's supposed to give the hospital three weeks' notice. I'll consider her as having resigned as of now, and start looking for somebody to replace her. That'll only leave her five days to go after you get home, and she'll survive that.'

'Wait a minute,' Bill said, his voice sobering abruptly. 'Do you think it's a good idea for her to quit? She loves staff work, and she's been happy there. I could see it in her every time she came over here.'

'I know she has, but there's no use considering it one way or the other. She'll quit, and that's that. You know it as well as I do.'

'But is staying home going to be enough for her, now she's had a taste of being back in harness again?'

'I don't know,' Kit said honestly. 'After all, that's up to her – and you.'

'It's up to her,' Bill said.

'Then there's no use worrying about it, is there?'

'No, I suppose not,' he admitted.

'Well, then – Oh, listen – may I tell Veazie Ann?'

'By all means. Tell her I want a big roast-beef dinner.'

'I'll tell her,' Kit promised. 'I'm happy, too, Bill.'

'Same here. See you soon.'

This conversation was the reason why, at the end of the following week, Sue found the next week's time sheet inexplicable. She had asked for the thirteenth and fourteenth off – the first to visit Bill and make some preparation for St Valentine's Day for the children, and the second to be at home with them. Instead, she was down for the fourteenth and fifteenth.

Sue thought perhaps Miss Patton had misunderstood,

but Miss Patton hadn't. The young Supervisor looked owlishly at Sue through red harlequin glasses, and was peculiarly and unreasonably obstinate.

'I'm terribly sorry, Mrs Barry,' she said, 'but I just can't change it now.'

That was that. Not that it mattered desperately, Sue realized. After all, she could go over to see Bill on the fifteenth. It was just that she had planned to have a party of some kind for the children, and there would now be no time to prepare for it.

'Oh, well,' Sue told Pat, 'they'll survive without a party this year.'

'I don't get it,' Pat said. 'I've gone all over that time sheet since you mentioned it, and I can't find a reason in the world why she shouldn't give you the days off you wanted, especially as you almost never ask for any particular time off.'

'Time sheets,' said Sue, remembering, 'can be awful. There's probably more in this than meets the eye.'

She accepted the change, since there was nothing else she could do, and a kindly Providence settled the matter of the party. There was, it turned out, to be one at school, and the children were far more excited about it than if it had been at home.

That'll larn me, Sue told herself, and when Kit announced that she was spending the night of the thirteenth and all day of the fourteenth in the bosom of the Barry family, Sue was delighted.

'If it's a nice day,' she said, 'we could go somewhere.'

But it was not, to Kit's relief, a nice day at all. It was a horrible day, foggy and dreary, with dirty wet patches of snow wherever one wished to step.

'Let's just stay home,' Kit said, curling up again in bed. Sue agreed wearily, and went downstairs to see what needed to be done. To her surprise, she found an immense roast of beef, just taken from the freezer, reposing on the kitchen table. She had been saving that roast until Bill's return. 'I'm sure I told Veazie Ann about it,' she muttered, and put the roast back in the freezer.

A short time afterwards Veazie Ann, who had been tidying up the children's rooms, came down to the kitchen, found the roast vanished, removed it from the freezer again, and put it back on the kitchen table. Then she went upstairs.

Sue, with the baby under her arm, came out to the kitchen, saw the roast, and returned it to the freezer. This inane performance might have gone on for some time, to the detriment of the roast, if Sue hadn't caught Veazie Ann bringing it out for the third time.

'Look,' Sue said, 'I hate to spoil your plans, Veazie Ann, but I was saving that roast for Bill.'

Veazie Ann choked. 'Sakes!' she said. 'I must of swallered something. But ye know, Sue, that roast had ought to be used. Them things get freezer-burn, or whatever 'tis ye call it, if ye leave 'em in too long.'

'But that hasn't been in more than three months. It couldn't possibly have a burn.'

'But ye don't know when Bill will be a-coming home,' said Veazie Ann desperately. 'Ye could git another, Sue. Honest – poor Kit, over there eating them hospital victuals all the time. Why don't we have a bang-up dinner tonight, for once in a way?'

'Oh, all right,' the disappointed Sue conceded, telling herself that, after all, one couldn't really go on living so far ahead – and why not have a swell dinner? Kit *would* love it.

Kit came downstairs about eleven o'clock and not, to Sue's surprise, in her oldest clothes. She looked, in fact, unusually smart.

'Mercy!' said Sue. 'What are you all dressed up for?'

'I'm not in the least dressed up,' said Kit indignantly. 'This is just an old thing.'

'It is not! I know just when you got it.'

'Well,' said Kit lamely, 'it's St Valentine's Day, and you never know who may be coming in.'

'Nobody's going to be coming in on a day like this,' Sue yawned, tousled her curls, and said, 'I'll tell you what, why don't we go to the movies this afternoon? It's ages since I've been.'

'Er – Well, let's see after lunch, shall we?'

Kit looked at Sue's old slacks and older blouse, and tried to think of some way to get her out of them. She also tried, and failed, to think of some way to make Sue forget about going to the movies.

'What'll I do with her?' Kit asked Veazie Ann, whom she caught alone for a moment in the kitchen. 'She's possessed of devils!'

'Jest be firm, that's all ye can do.'

'Well, I'll try – but it's going to be worse after lunch.'

It was. Lunch was at one o'clock, and promptly afterwards Sue took the baby upstairs for a nap. When she returned to the living-room she said briskly, 'Now, what about the movies?'

Kit moaned.

'I don't know what's got into you,' said Sue, a little crossly. 'Why not go? It's a miserable day, and Veazie Ann is here to look after the kids.'

Kit saw that Veazie Ann had been right. Firm measures were necessary.

'I don't care who's going to look after the kids,' she said. 'I'm exhausted and I'd like to rest, in a real house, with a fire in the fireplace, and dinner smelling gorgeous in the oven. I definitely will *not* go to any damp smelly movies. I should think *you* could understand what it means to have a chance to stay at home once in a while.'

Sue was instantly contrite. 'Of course, I understand, Kitten. We'll just settle down and relax.' To prove her good intentions, Sue curled up in an easy chair, stared at the fire for a few minutes, and then said dreamily, 'This would be a lovely afternoon to clean the attic. No – you needn't look so horrified. This is a one-woman job. You stay right here and rest.'

'Look,' Kit said faintly, 'can't we *both* stay right here and rest?'

Sue was beginning to be puzzled. She was also somewhat frustrated. She and Kit had never interfered with one another, and it seemed to her that Kit's behaviour was definitely peculiar. But, after all, it was no cinch to be a Director of Nurses. Poor Kitty. Her nerves were probably on edge. That could give you an attack of the 'no's'. Sue abandoned the attic without further struggle.

'What would *you* like to do?' she asked gently.

'Oh, just lie here on the couch, and talk, and maybe have some tea by and by.'

'All right – let's,' said the generous Sue, and Kit relaxed.

They talked, remembering old times, old friends, and old adventures, and the time passed quickly enough, though Kit had still been unable to think of any way to get Sue into one of her more charming housecoats. Well, it probably didn't matter. Sue's hair always looked gorgeous, and Bill would undoubtedly not care what she had on.

At a little after three the children came home from school laden with valentines, candy, and practically all the dirty snow in the White Mountains, or so it seemed to Kit.

Veazie Ann made short work of the snow, the sticky hands and faces, and the rumpled hair.

'Now then,' she said firmly, 'go and play quietly in the living-room.'

They played quietly enough, but Johnny set up his electric train in the front hall where Bill would be certain to trip over it, provided he could get the door open at all. Tabitha settled herself on the rug in front of the fire with a stack of old magazines and a pair of scissors and prepared to spend a pleasant afternoon cutting out paper dolls. How she managed to cover a large portion of the entire room with little snips of paper, Kit didn't know, but in any case the room was beginning to assume an appallingly littered appearance which could hardly be restful to a man just home from the orderly life of a sanatorium – and tired from the trip. Jerry added to the effect by dumping a large box of assorted and very dirty stones all over the remaining clear space. Sue, in and out of the room on various household errands, didn't seem to notice the general mess at all.

'Johnny,' Kit suggested tentatively, 'don't you want to put your electric train things on the dining-room floor – or – or somewhere?'

'Oh, they have their toys all over the place,' said Sue comfortably from the kitchen doorway. There was a smudge of soot on her chin. 'Remember,' she added, 'they're very good about putting their things away.'

Kit gave up. If Sue had known, she would, of course, have had everything, including the children, spick-and-span. But she didn't know, and Kit couldn't tell her. Or had Sue changed? It was hard to say.

Tabitha, always sensitive beneath her matter-of-fact exterior, rose suddenly in a shower of paper, and came to lean against the arm of Kit's chair.

'What are you thinking about, Aunt Kit?' she demanded.

'Why?' Kit countered.

'Because you look sort of funny – sad – and kind of worried.'

'I'm not a bit worried, dear, and I wasn't thinking anything special – just scrambled things. Don't you, sometimes?'

'Oh, yes!' said Tabitha, relieved. 'Lots of times I –'

Sue came briskly into the room, a dish towel dangling from one hand. '*I* think,' she said, 'that we could all do with some tea and hot gingerbread. What do you –'

The sentence was never finished for at that moment the front door opened, cautiously, and Bill stood for a moment, his tall figure framed in the open doorway against the snowy mountains in the distance. Then he stepped with the skill of long practice over the tracks and trains on the floor and paused on the living-room threshold, looking at the familiar room and its litter of toys. In the brief moment before the stunned Sue could speak, before a screaming Johnny could attach himself to his father's leg, before pandemonium broke loose, Kit saw Bill's quick eyes taking in the paper snips, the stones, the dish towel in Sue's hand, and the smudge on her chin. There was a deep and abiding satisfaction in his eyes.

When all the uproar had subsided, when all the explanations had been made, when Bill was settled at last in his own chair before the fire, with the half-awake baby in his arms, the children breathing down his neck, and Sue leaning on his chair back, one hand resting lightly on his shoulder as if to make sure that he were real, he grinned across at Kit. Then he winced, stirred uneasily, and groped behind him in the chair. What he produced, after a slight struggle, was a box filled with mildewed moss upon which reposed a tin soldier with very fixed bayonet.

'The sanatorium,' said Bill in utter contentment, 'was *never* like this!'